Rudyard Kipling

Soldier Tales

Rudyard Kipling

Soldier Tales

ISBN/EAN: 9783337023140

Printed in Europe, USA, Canada, Australia, Japan

Cover: Foto ©Andreas Hilbeck / pixelio.de

More available books at **www.hansebooks.com**

BY

RUDYARD KIPLING

𝔏𝔬𝔫𝔡𝔬𝔫
MACMILLAN AND CO., Lᴛᴅ.
NEW YORK: THE MACMILLAN CO.
1896

CONTENTS

LIST OF ILLUSTRATIONS

WITH THE MAIN GUARD

Der jungere Uhlanen
Sit round mit open mouth
While Breitmann tell dem stdories
Of fightin' in the South ;
Und gif dem moral lessons,
How before der battle pops,
Take a little prayer to Himmel
Und a goot long drink of Schnapps.
Hans Breitmann's Ballads.

'MARY, Mother av Mercy, fwhat the divil possist us to take an' kape this melancolious counthry?   Answer me that, Sorr.'

It was Mulvaney who was speaking.   The time was one o'clock of a stifling June night, and the place was the main gate of Fort Amara, most desolate and least desirable of all fortresses in India.   What I was doing there at that hour is a question which only concerns M'Grath the Sergeant of the Guard, and the men on the gate.

'Slape,' said Mulvaney, 'is a shuparfluous necessity. This gyard'll shtay lively till relieved.'   He himself was stripped to the waist ; Learoyd on the next bedstead was dripping from the skinful of water which Ortheris, clad only in white trousers, had just sluiced over his shoulders ; and a fourth private was muttering

𝔈   B

uneasily as he dozed open-mouthed in the glare of the great guard-lantern. The heat under the bricked archway was terrifying.

'The worrst night that iver I remimber. Eyah! Is all Hell loose this tide?' said Mulvaney. A puff of burning wind lashed through the wicket-gate like a wave of the sea, and Ortheris swore.

'Are ye more heasy, Jock?' he said to Learoyd. 'Put yer 'ead between your legs. It'll go orf in a minute.'

'Ah don't care. Ah would not care, but ma heart is plaayin' tivvy-tivvy on ma ribs. Let me die! Oh, leave me die!' groaned the huge York-shireman, who was feeling the heat acutely, being of fleshly build.

The sleeper under the lantern roused for a moment and raised himself on his elbow.—'Die and be damned then!' he said. '*I*'m damned and I can't die!'

'Who's that?' I whispered, for the voice was new to me.

'Gentleman born,' said Mulvaney; 'Corp'ril wan year, Sargint nex'. Red-hot on his C'mission, but dhrinks like a fish. He'll be gone before the cowld weather's here. So!'

He slipped his boot, and with the naked toe just touched the trigger of his Martini. Ortheris misunderstood the movement, and the next instant the Irishman's rifle was dashed aside, while Ortheris stood before him, his eyes blazing with reproof.

'You!' said Ortheris. 'My Gawd, *you!* If it was you, wot would *we* do?'

'Kape quiet, little man,' said Mulvaney, putting him aside, but very gently; ''tis not me, nor will ut

'Put yer 'ead between your legs. It'll go orf in a minute.'—P. 2.

be me whoile Dinah Shadd's here. I was but showin' something.'

Learoyd, bowed on his bedstead, groaned, and the gentleman-ranker sighed in his sleep. Ortheris took Mulvaney's tendered pouch, and we three smoked gravely for a space while the dust-devils danced on the glacis and scoured the red-hot plain.

'Pop?' said Ortheris, wiping his forehead.

'Don't tantalise wid talkin' av dhrink, or I'll shtuff you into your own breech-block an'—fire you off!' grunted Mulvaney.

Ortheris chuckled, and from a niche in the veranda produced six bottles of gingerade.

'Where did ye get ut, ye Machiavel?' said Mulvaney. ''Tis no bazar pop.'

''Ow do *Hi* know wot the Orf'cers drink?' answered Ortheris. 'Arst the mess-man.'

'Ye'll have a Disthrict Coort-Martial settin' on ye yet, me son,' said Mulvaney, 'but'—he opened a bottle—'I will not report ye this time. Fwhat's in the mess-kid is mint for the belly, as they say, 'specially whin that mate is dhrink. Here's luck! A bloody war or a—no, we've got the sickly season. War, thin!'—he waved the innocent 'pop' to the four quarters of Heaven. 'Bloody war! North, East, South, an' West! Jock, ye quakin' hayrick, come an' dhrink.'

But Learoyd, half mad with the fear of death presaged in the swelling veins of his neck, was begging his Maker to strike him dead, and fighting for more air between his prayers. A second time Ortheris drenched the quivering body with water, and the giant revived.

'An' Ah divn't see thot a mon is i' fettle for gooin' on to live; an' Ah divn't see thot there is owt for t' livin' for. Hear now, lads! Ah'm tired —tired. There's nobbut watter i' ma bones. Let me die!'

The hollow of the arch gave back Learoyd's broken whisper in a bass boom. Mulvaney looked at me hopelessly, but I remembered how the madness of despair had once fallen upon Ortheris, that weary, weary afternoon in the banks of the Khemi River, and how it had been exorcised by the skilful magician Mulvaney.

'Talk, Terence!' I said, 'or we shall have Learoyd slinging loose, and he'll be worse than Ortheris was. Talk! He'll answer to your voice.'

Almost before Ortheris had deftly thrown all the rifles of the guard on Mulvaney's bedstead, the Irishman's voice was uplifted as that of one in the middle of a story, and, turning to me, he said—

'In barricks or out of it, as *you* say, Sorr, an Oirish rig'mint is the divil an' more. 'Tis only fit for a young man wid eddicated fisteses. Oh the crame av disruption is an Oirish rig'mint, an' rippin', tearin', ragin' scattherers in the field av war! My first rig'mint was Oirish—Faynians an' rebils to the heart av their marrow was they, an' *so* they fought for the Widdy betther than most, bein' contrairy— Oirish. They was the Black Tyrone. You've heard av thim, Sorr?'

Heard of them! I knew the Black Tyrone for the choicest collection of unmitigated blackguards, dog-stealers, robbers of hen-roosts, assaulters of in-

nocent citizens, and recklessly daring heroes in the
Army List. Half Europe and half Asia has had
cause to know the Black Tyrone—good luck be with
their tattered Colours as Glory has ever been!

'They *was* hot pickils an' ginger! I cut a man's
head tu deep wid my belt in the days av my youth,
an', afther some circumstances which I will oblithe-
rate, I came to the Ould Rig'mint, bearin' the character av a man wid hands an' feet. But, as I was
goin' to tell you, I fell acrost the Black Tyrone
agin wan day whin we wanted thim powerful bad.
Orth'ris, me son, fwhat was the name av that place
where they sint wan comp'ny av us an' wan av the
Tyrone roun' a hill an' down again, all for to tache
the Paythans something they'd niver learned before?
Afther Ghuzni 'twas.'

'Don't know what the bloomin' Paythans called
it. We called it Silver's Theayter. You know that,
sure!'

'Silver's Theatre—so 'twas. A gut betune two
hills, as black as a bucket, an' as thin as a girl's
waist. There was over-many Paythans for our con-
vaynience in the gut, an' begad they called thimselves
a Reserve—bein' impident by natur! Our Scotchies
an' lashins av Gurkys was poundin' into some Paythan rig'ments, I think 'twas. Scotchies and Gurkys
are twins bekaze they're so onlike, an' they get
dhrunk together whin God plazes. As I was sayin',
they sint wan comp'ny av the Ould an' wan av the
Tyrone to double up the hill an' clane out the Paythan Reserve. Orf'cers was scarce in thim days,
fwhat wid dysintry an' not takin' care av thimselves,
an' we was sint out wid only wan orf'cer for the

comp'ny ; but he was a Man that had his feet beneath him, an' all his teeth in their sockuts.'

'Who was he?' I asked.

'Captain O'Neil—Old Crook—Cruikna-bulleen
—him that I tould ye that tale av whin he was in
Burma.[1]   Hah!   He was a Man.   The Tyrone tuk
a little orf'cer bhoy, but divil a bit was he in command,
as I'll dimonstrate presintly.   We an' they came over
the brow av the hill, wan on each side av the gut, an'
there was that ondacint Reserve waitin' down below
like rats in a pit.

' " Howld on, men," sez Crook, who tuk a mother's
care av us always.   " Rowl some rocks on thim by
way av visitin'-kyards."   We hadn't rowled more
than twinty bowlders, an' the Paythans was beginnin' to swear tremenjus, whin the little orf'cer bhoy
av the Tyrone shqueaks out acrost the valley :—
"Fwhat the devil an' all are you doin', shpoilin' the
fun for my men ?   Do ye not see they'll stand ? "

' " Faith, that's a rare pluckt wan ! " sez Crook.
" Niver mind the rocks, men.   Come along down an'
take tay wid thim ! "

' " There's damned little sugar in ut ! " sez my
rear-rank man ; but Crook heard.

' " Have ye not all got spoons ? " he sez, laughin',
an' down we wint as fast as we cud.   Learoyd bein'
sick at the Base, he, av coorse, was not there.'

'Thot's a lie ! ' said Learoyd, dragging his bedstead nearer.   ' Ah gotten *thot* theer, an' you knaw
it, Mulvaney.'   He threw up his arms, and from the

---

[1] Now first of the foemen of Boh Da Thone
Was Captain O'Neil of the Black Tyrone.
The Ballad of Boh Da Thone.

right arm-pit ran, diagonally through the fell of his chest, a thin white line terminating near the fourth left rib.

' My mind's goin',' said Mulvaney, the unabashed. ' Ye were there. Fwhat was I thinkin' of ? 'Twas another man, av coorse. Well, you'll remimber thin, Jock, how we an' the Tyrone met wid a bang at the bottom an' got jammed past all movin' among the Paythans ? '

' Ow! It *was* a tight 'ole. I was squeezed till I thought I'd bloomin' well bust,' said Ortheris, rubbing his stomach meditatively.

' 'Twas no place for a little man, but *wan* little man '—Mulvaney put his hand on Ortheris's shoulder —' saved the life av me. There we shtuck, for divil a bit did the Paythans flinch, an' divil a bit dare we; our business bein' to clear 'em out. An' the most exthryordinar' thing av all was that we an' they just rushed into each other's arrums, an' there was no firing for a long time. Nothin' but knife an' bay'nit when we cud get our hands free : an' that was not often. We was breast-on to thim, an' the Tyrone was yelpin' behind av us in a way I didn't see the lean av at first. But I knew later, an' so did the Paythans.

' " Knee to knee! " sings out Crook, wid a laugh whin the rush av our comin' into the gut shtopped, an' he was huggin' a hairy great Paythan, neither bein' able to do anything to the other, tho' both was wishful.

' " Breast to breast! " he sez, as the Tyrone was pushin' us forward closer an' closer.

' " An' hand over back! " sez a Sargint that was

behin'. I saw a sword lick out past Crook's ear, an'
the Paythan was tuk in the apple av his throat like
a pig at Dromeen Fair.

'"Thank ye, Brother Inner Guard," sez Crook,
cool as a cucumber widout salt. "I wanted that
room." An' he wint forward by the thickness av a
man's body, havin' turned the Paythan undher him.
The man bit the heel off Crook's boot in his death-
bite.

'"Push, men!" sez Crook. "Push, ye paper-
backed beggars!" he sez. "Am I to pull ye
through?" So we pushed, an' we kicked, an' we
swung, an' we swore, an' the grass bein' slippery
our heels wouldn't bite, an' God help the front-rank
man that wint down that day!'

''Ave you ever bin in the Pit hentrance o' the
Vic. on a thick night?' interrupted Ortheris. 'It
was worse nor that, for they was goin' one way, an'
we wouldn't 'ave it. Leastaways, I 'adn't much to
say.'

'Faith, me son, ye said ut, thin. I kep' the little
man betune my knees as long as I cud, but he was
pokin' roun' wid his bay'nit, blindin' and stiffin'
feroshus. The devil of a man is Orth'ris in a ruction
—aren't ye?' said Mulvaney.

'Don't make game!' said the Cockney. 'I
knowed I wasn't no good then, but I guv 'em compot
from the lef' flank when we opened out. No!' he
said, bringing down his hand with a thump on the
bedstead, ' a bay'nit ain't no good to a little man—
might as well 'ave a bloomin' fishin'-rod! I 'ate a
clawin', maulin' mess, but gimme a breech that's wore
out a bit, an' hamminition one year in store, to let the

powder kiss the bullet, an' put me somewheres where I ain't trod on by 'ulkin' swine like you, an' s'elp me Gawd, I could bowl you over five times outer seven at height 'undred. Would yer try, you lumberin' Hirishman?'

'No, ye wasp. I've seen ye do ut. I say there's nothin' better than the bay'nit, wid a long reach, a double twist av ye can, an' a slow recover.'

'Dom the bay'nit,' said Learoyd, who had been listening intently. 'Look a-here!' He picked up a rifle an inch below the foresight with an underhanded action, and used it exactly as a man would use a dagger.

'Sitha,' said he softly, 'thot's better than owt, for a mon can bash t' faace wi' thot, an', if he divn't, he can breeak t' forearm o' t' gaard. 'Tis not i' t' books, though. Gie me t' butt.'

'Each does ut his own way, like makin' love,' said Mulvaney quietly; 'the butt or the bay'nit or the bullet accordin' to the natur' av the man. Well, as I was sayin', we shtuck there breathin' in each other's faces an' swearin' powerful; Orth'ris cursin' the mother that bore him bekaze he was not three inches taller.

'Prisintly he sez :—" Duck, ye lump, an' I can get at a man over your shouldher!"

'" You'll blow me head off," I sez, throwin' my arm clear ; " go through under my arm-pit, ye blood-thirsty little scutt," sez I, " but don't shtick me or I'll wring your ears round."

'Fwhat was ut ye gave the Paythan man forninst me, him that cut at me whin I cudn't move hand or foot? Hot or cowld was ut?'

'Cold,' said Ortheris, 'up an' under the rib-jint. 'E come down flat. Best for you 'e did.'

'Thrue, my son! This jam thing that I'm talkin' about lasted for five minutes good, an' thin we got our arms clear an' wint in. I misremimber exactly fwhat I did, but I didn't want Dinah to be a widdy at the Depot. Thin, after some promishkuous hackin' we shtuck again, an' the Tyrone behin' was callin' us dogs an' cowards an' all manner av names; we barrin' their way.

'"Fwhat ails the Tyrone?" thinks I; "they've the makin's av a most convanient fight here."

'A man behind me sez beseechful an' in a whisper: —"Let me get at thim! For the love av Mary give me room beside ye, ye tall man!"

'"An' who are you that's so anxious to be kilt?" sez I, widout turnin' my head, for the long knives was dancin' in front like the sun on Donegal Bay whin ut's rough.

'"We've seen our dead," he sez, squeezin' into me; "our dead that was men two days gone! An' me that was his cousin by blood could not bring Tim Coulan off! Let me get on," he sez, "let me get to thim or I'll run ye through the back!"

'"My troth," thinks I, "if the Tyrone have seen their dead, God help the Paythans this day!" An' thin I knew why the Oirish was ragin' behind us as they was.

'I gave room to the man, an' he ran forward wid the Haymakers' Lift on his bay'nit an' swung a Paythan clear off his feet by the belly-band av the brute, an' the iron bruk at the lockin'-ring.

'"Tim Coulan 'll slape easy to-night," sez he wid

a grin ; an' the next minut his head was in two halves and he wint down grinnin' by sections.

'The Tyrone was pushin' an' pushin' in, an' our men was swearin' at thim, an' Crook was workin' away in front av us all, his sword-arm swingin' like a pump-handle an' his revolver spittin' like a cat. But the strange thing av ut was the quiet that lay upon. 'Twas like a fight in a drame—except for thim that was dead.

'Whin I gave room to the Oirishman I was ex-pinded an' forlorn in my inside. 'Tis a way I have, savin' your presince, Sorr, in action. " Let me out, bhoys," sez I, backin' in among thim. " I'm goin' to be onwell !" Faith they gave me room at the wurrd, though they would not ha' given room for all Hell wid the chill off. When I got clear, I was, savin' your presince, Sorr, outragis sick bekaze I had dhrunk heavy that day.

'Well an' far out av harm was a Sargint av the Tyrone sittin' on the little orf'cer bhoy who had stopped Crook from rowlin' the rocks. Oh, he was a beautiful bhoy, an' the long black curses was sliding out av his innocint mouth like mornin'-jew from a rose !

'" Fwhat have you got there ? " sez I to the Sargint.

'" Wan av Her Majesty's bantams wid his spurs up," sez he. " He's goin' to Coort-Martial me."

'" Let me go ! " sez the little orf'cer bhoy. " Let me go and command my men !" manin' thereby the Black Tyrone which was beyond any command—ay, even av they had made the Divil a Field-Orf'cer.

'" His father howlds my mother's cow-feed in

Clonmel," sez the man that was sittin' on him. "Will I go back to *his* mother an' tell her that I've let him throw himself away? Lie still, ye little pinch av dynamite, an' Coort-Martial me aftherwards."

' " Good," sez I ; " 'tis the likes av him makes the likes av the Commandher-in-Chief, but we must presarve thim. Fwhat d'you want to do, Sorr ? " sez I, very politeful.

' " Kill the beggars — kill the beggars ! " he shqueaks, his big blue eyes brimmin' wid tears.

' " An' how'll ye do that ? " sez I. " You've shquibbed off your revolver like a child wid a cracker ; you can make no play wid that fine large sword av yours ; an' your hand's shakin' like an asp on a leaf. Lie still and grow," sez I.

' " Get back to your comp'ny," sez he ; " you're insolint ! "

' " All in good time," sez I, " but I'll have a dhrink first."

' Just thin Crook comes up, blue an' white all over where he wasn't red.

' " Wather ! " sez he ; " I'm dead wid drouth ! Oh, but it's a gran' day ! "

' He dhrank half a skinful, and the rest he tilts into his chest, an' it fair hissed on the hairy hide av him. He sees the little orf'cer bhoy undher the Sargint.

' " Fwhat's yonder ? " sez he.

' " Mutiny, Sorr," sez the Sargint, an' the orf'cer bhoy begins pleadin' pitiful to Crook to be let go : but divil a bit wud Crook budge.

' " Kape him there," he sez, " 'tis no child's work

this day. By the same token," sez he, " I'll confish-
cate that iligant nickel - plated scent-sprinkler av
yours, for my own has been vomitin' dishgraceful ! "

'The fork av his hand was black wid the back-
spit av the machine. So he tuk the orf'cer bhoy's
revolver. Ye may look, Sorr, but, by my faith,
*there's a dale more done in the field than iver gets into
Field Ordhers !*

'"Come on, Mulvaney," sez Crook ; "is this a
Coort-Martial ? " The two av us wint back together
into the mess an' the Paythans were still standin' up.
They was not *too* impart'nint though, for the Tyrone
was callin' wan to another to remimber Tim Coulan.

'Crook stopped outside av the strife an' looked
anxious, his eyes rowlin' roun'.

'"Fwhat is ut, Sorr?" sez I ; "can I get ye
anything ? "

'"Where's a bugler ? " sez he.

'I wint into the crowd—our men was dhrawin'
breath behin' the Tyrone who was fightin' like sowls
in tormint—an' prisintly I came acrost little Frehan,
our bugler bhoy, pokin' roun' among the best wid a
rifle an' bay'nit.

'"Is amusin' yoursilf fwhat you're paid for, ye
limb?" sez I, catchin' him by the scruff. "Come
out av that an' attind to your duty," I sez ; but the
bhoy was not pleased.

'"I've got wan," sez he, grinnin', "big as you,
Mulvaney, an' fair half as ugly. Let me go get
another."

'I was dishpleased at the personability av that
remark, so I tucks him under my arm an' carries
him to Crook who was watchin' how the fight wint.

Crook cuffs him till the bhoy cries, an' thin sez
nothin' for a whoile.

'The Paythans began to flicker onaisy, an' our
men roared. "Opin ordher! Double!" sez Crook.
"Blow, child, blow for the honour av the British
Arrmy!"

'That bhoy blew like a typhoon, an' the Tyrone
an' we opined out as the Paythans broke, an' I saw
that fwhat had gone before wud be kissin' an'
huggin' to fwhat was to come. We'd dhruv thim
into a broad part av the gut whin they gave, an'
thin we opined out an' fair danced down the valley,
dhrivin' thim before us. Oh, 'twas lovely, an' stiddy,
too! There was the Sargints on the flanks av what
was left av us, kapin' touch, an' the fire was runnin'
from flank to flank, an' the Paythans was dhroppin'.
We opined out wid the widenin' av the valley, an'
whin the valley narrowed we closed again like the
shticks on a lady's fan, an' at the far ind av the gut
where they thried to stand, we fair blew them off
their feet, for we had expinded very little ammunition by reason av the knife work.'

'Hi used thirty rounds goin' down that valley,'
said Ortheris, 'an' it was gentleman's work. Might
'a' done it in a white 'andkerchief an' pink silk
stockin's, that part. Hi was on in that piece.'

'You could ha' heard the Tyrone yellin' a mile
away,' said Mulvaney, 'an' 'twas all their Sargints
cud do to get thim off. They was mad — mad
—mad! Crook sits down in the quiet that fell
when we had gone down the valley, an' covers his
face wid his hands. Prisintly we all came back
again accordin' to our natures and disposishins, for

they, mark you, show through the hide av a man in
that hour.

'"Bhoys! bhoys!" sez Crook to himself. "I
misdoubt we could ha' engaged at long range an'
saved betther men than me." He looked at our
dead an' said no more.

'"Captain dear," sez a man av the Tyrone,
comin' up wid his mouth bigger than iver his mother
kissed ut, spittin' blood like a whale; "Captain
dear," sez he, "if wan or two in the shtalls have
been discommoded, the gallery have enjoyed the
performinces av a Roshus."

'Thin I knew that man for the Dublin dock-rat
he was—wan av the bhoys that made the lessee av
Silver's Theatre gray before his time wid tearin' out
the bowils av the benches an' t'rowin' thim into the
pit. So I passed the wurrud that I knew when
I was in the Tyrone an' we lay in Dublin. "I
don't know who 'twas," I whispers, "an' I don't
care, but anyways I'll knock the face av you, Tim
Kelly."

'"Eyah!" sez the man, "was you there too?
We'll call ut Silver's Theatre." .Half the Tyrone,
knowin' the ould place, tuk ut up: so we called ut
Silver's Theatre.

'The little orf'cer bhoy av the Tyrone was
thremblin' an' cryin'. He had no heart for the Coort-
Martials that he talked so big upon. "Ye'll do well
later," sez Crook, very quiet, "for not bein' allowed
to kill yourself for amusemint."

'"I'm a dishgraced man!" sez the little orf'cer
bhoy.

'"Put me undher arrest, Sorr, if you will, but,

by my sowl, I'd do ut again sooner than face your mother wid you dead," sez the Sargint that had sat on his head, standin' to attention an' salutin'. But the young wan only cried as tho' his little heart was breakin'.

'Thin another man av the Tyrone came up, wid the fog av fightin' on him.'

'The what, Mulvaney?'

'Fog av fightin'. You know, Sorr, that, like makin' love, ut takes each man diff'rint. Now I can't help bein' powerful sick whin I'm in action. Orth'ris, here, niver stops swearin' from ind to ind, an' the only time that Learoyd opins his mouth to sing is whin he is messin' wid other people's heads; for he's a dhirty fighter is Jock. Recruities some-time cry, an' sometime they don't know fwhat they do, an' sometime they are all for cuttin' throats an' such-like dirtiness; but some men get heavy-dead-dhrunk on the fightin'. This man was. He was staggerin', an' his eyes were half-shut, an' we cud hear him dhraw breath twinty yards away. He sees the little orf'cer bhoy, an' comes up, talkin' thick an' drowsy to himsilf. "Blood the young whelp!" he sez; "blood the young whelp"; an' wid that he threw up his arms, shpun roun', an' dropped at our feet, dead as a Paythan, an' there was niver sign or scratch on him. They said 'twas his heart was rotten, but oh, 'twas a quare thing to see!

'Thin we wint to bury our dead, for we wud not lave them to the Paythans, an' in movin' among the haythen we nearly lost that little orf'cer bhoy. He was for givin' wan divil wather and layin' him aisy against a rock. "Be careful, Sorr," sez I; "a

wounded Paythan's worse than a live wan." My
troth, before the words was out of my mouth, the
man on the ground fires at the orf'cer bhoy lanin'
over him, an' I saw the helmit fly. I dropped the
butt on the face av the man an' tuk his pistol. The
little orf'cer bhoy turned very white, for the hair av
half his head was singed away.

'"I tould you so, Sorr," sez I ; an', afther that,
whin he wanted to help a Paythan I stud wid the
muzzle contagious to the ear. They dare not do
anythin' but curse. The Tyrone was growlin' like
dogs over a bone that has been taken away too
soon, for they had seen their dead an' they wanted
to kill ivry sowl on the ground. Crook tould thim
that he'd blow the hide off any man that miscon-
ducted himself ; but, seeing that ut was the first
time the Tyrone had iver seen their dead, I do not
wondher they were on the sharp. 'Tis a shameful
sight ! Whin I first saw ut I wud niver ha' given
quarter to any man north of the Khaibar—no, nor
woman either, for the women used to come out
afther dhark—Auggrh !

'Well, evenshually we buried our dead an' tuk
away our wounded, an' come over the brow av the
hills to see the Scotchies an' the Gurkys taking tay
with the Paythans in bucketsfuls. We were a gang
av dissolute ruffians, for the blood had caked the
dust, an' the sweat had cut the cake, an' our bay'nits
was hangin' like butchers' steels betune ur legs, an'
most av us were marked one way or another.

'A Staff Orf'cer man, clean as a new rifle, rides
up an' sez : "What damned scarecrows are you ? "

'"A comp'ny av Her Majesty's Black Tyrone an'
C

wan av the Ould Rig'mint," sez Crook very quiet, givin' our visitors the flure as 'twas.

'"Oh!" sez the Staff Orf'cer; "did you dislodge that Reserve?"

'"No!" sez Crook, an' the Tyrone laughed.

'"Thin fwhat the divil have ye done?"

'"Disthroyed ut," sez Crook, an' he took us on, but not before Toomey that was in the Tyrone sez aloud, his voice somewhere in his stummick: "Fwhat in the name av misfortune does this parrit widout a tail mane by shtoppin' the road av his betthers?"

'The Staff Orf'cer wint blue, an' Toomey makes him pink by changin' to the voice av a minowderin' woman an' sayin': "Come an' kiss me, Major dear, for me husband's at the wars an' I'm all alone at the Depot."

'The Staff Orf'cer wint away, an' I cud see Crook's shoulthers shakin'.

'His Corp'ril checks Toomey. "Lave me alone," sez Toomey, widout a wink. "I was his bâtman before he was married an' he knows fwhat I mane, av you don't. There's nothin' like livin' in the hoight av society." D'you remimber that, Orth'ris?'

'Hi do. Toomey, 'e died in 'orspital, next week it was, 'cause I bought 'arf his kit; an' I remember after that——'

'GUARRD, TURN OUT!'

The Relief had come; it was four o'clock. 'I'll catch a kyart for you, Sorr,' said Mulvaney, diving hastily into his accoutrements. 'Come up to the top av the Fort an' we'll pershue our invistigations into M'Grath's shtable.' The relieved guard strolled round the main bastion on its way to the swimming-

He picked her up in the growing light, and set her on his shoulder.—P. 19.

bath, and Learoyd grew almost talkative. Ortheris
looked into the Fort ditch and across the plain.
'Ho! it's weary waitin' for Ma-ary!' he hummed;
'but I'd like to kill some more bloomin' Paythans
before my time's up. War! Bloody war! North,
East, South, and West.'

'Amen,' said Learoyd slowly.

'Fwhat's here?' said Mulvaney, checking at a
blur of white by the foot of the old sentry-box. He
stooped and touched it. 'It's Norah—Norah M'Taggart! Why, Nonie darlin', fwhat are ye doin' out
av your mother's bed at this time?'

The two-year-old child of Sergeant M'Taggart
must have wandered for a breath of cool air to the
very verge of the parapet of the Fort ditch. Her
tiny night-shift was gathered into a wisp round her
neck and she moaned in her sleep. 'See there!'
said Mulvaney; 'poor lamb! Look at the heat-rash
on the innocint skin av her. 'Tis hard—crool hard
even for us. Fwhat must it be for these? Wake
up, Nonie, your mother will be woild about you.
Begad, the child might ha' fallen into the ditch!'

He picked her up in the growing light, and set
her on his shoulder, and her fair curls touched the
grizzled stubble of his temples. Ortheris and Learoyd followed snapping their fingers, while Norah
smiled at them a sleepy smile. Then carolled
Mulvaney, clear as a lark, dancing the baby on
his arm—

'If any young man should marry you,
    Say nothin' about the joke;
That iver ye slep' in a sinthry-box,
    Wrapped up in a soldier's cloak.'

'Though, on my sowl, Nonie,' he said gravely, 'there was not much cloak about you. Niver mind, you won't dhress like this ten years to come. Kiss your friends an' run along to your mother.'

Nonie, set down close to the Married Quarters, nodded with the quiet obedience of the soldier's child, but, ere she pattered off over the flagged path, held up her lips to be kissed by the Three Musketeers. Ortheris wiped his mouth with the back of his hand and swore sentimentally; Learoyd turned pink; and the two walked away together. The Yorkshireman lifted up his voice and gave in thunder the chorus of *The Sentry-Box*, while Ortheris piped at his side.

''Bin to a bloomin' sing-song, you two?' said the Artilleryman, who was taking his cartridge down to the Morning Gun. 'You're over merry for these dashed days.'

> 'I bid ye take care o' the brat, said he,
> For it comes of a noble race,'

Learoyd bellowed. The voices died out in the swimming-bath.

'Oh, Terence!' I said, dropping into Mulvaney's speech, when we were alone, 'it's you that have the Tongue!'

He looked at me wearily; his eyes were sunk in his head, and his face was drawn and white. 'Eyah!' said he; 'I've blandandhered thim through the night somehow, but can thim that helps others help thimselves? Answer me that, Sorr!'

And over the bastions of Fort Amara broke the pitiless day.

THE DRUMS OF THE FORE AND AFT

IN the Army List they still stand as 'The Fore and
Fit Princess Hohenzollern-Sigmaringen-Auspach's
Merthyr-Tydfilshire Own Royal Loyal Light Infantry, Regimental District 329A,' but the Army
through all its barracks and canteens knows them
now as the 'Fore and Aft.' They may in time do
something that shall make their new title honourable,
but at present they are bitterly ashamed, and the
man who calls them 'Fore and Aft' does so at the
risk of the head which is on his shoulders.

Two words breathed into the stables of a certain
Cavalry Regiment will bring the men out into the
streets with belts and mops and bad language ; but
a whisper of 'Fore and Aft' will bring out this
regiment with rifles.

Their one excuse is that they came again and
did their best to finish the job in style. But for a
time all their world knows that they were openly
beaten, whipped, dumb-cowed, shaking, and afraid.
The men know it ; their officers know it ; the Horse
Guards know it, and when the next war comes the
enemy will know it also. There are two or three

regiments of the Line that have a black mark against their names which they will then wipe out; and it will be excessively inconvenient for the troops upon whom they do their wiping.

The courage of the British soldier is officially supposed to be above proof, and, as a general rule, it is so. The exceptions are decently shovelled out of sight, only to be referred to in the freshest of unguarded talk that occasionally swamps a Mess-table at midnight. Then one hears strange and horrible stories of men not following their officers, of orders being given by those who had no right to give them, and of disgrace that, but for the standing luck of the British Army, might have ended in brilliant disaster. These are unpleasant stories to listen to, and the Messes tell them under their breath, sitting by the big wood fires, and the young officer bows his head and thinks to himself, please God, his men shall never behave unhandily.

The British soldier is not altogether to be blamed for occasional lapses; but this verdict he should not know. A moderately intelligent General will waste six months in mastering the craft of the particular war that he may be waging; a Colonel may utterly misunderstand the capacity of his regiment for three months after it has taken the field; and even a Company Commander may err and be deceived as to the temper and temperament of his own handful: wherefore the soldier, and the soldier of to-day more particularly, should not be blamed for falling back. He should be shot or hanged afterwards—to encourage the others; but he should not be vilified in news-papers, for that is want of tact and waste of space.

He has, let us say, been in the service of the
Empress for, perhaps, four years. He will leave in
another two years. He has no inherited morals, and
four years are not sufficient to drive toughness into
his fibre, or to teach him how holy a thing is his Regiment. He wants to drink, he wants to enjoy himself—in India he wants to save money—and he does
not in the least like getting hurt. He has received
just sufficient education to make him understand
half the purport of the orders he receives, and to
speculate on the nature of clean, incised, and shatter-
ing wounds. Thus, if he is told to deploy under fire
preparatory to an attack, he knows that he runs a
very great risk of being killed while he is deploy-
ing, and suspects that he is being thrown away to
gain ten minutes' time. He may either deploy with
desperate swiftness, or he may shuffle, or bunch, or
break, according to the discipline under which he has
lain for four years.

Armed with imperfect knowledge, cursed with
the rudiments of an imagination, hampered by the
intense selfishness of the lower classes, and unsupported by any regimental associations, this young
man is suddenly introduced to an enemy who in
eastern lands is always ugly, generally tall and hairy,
and frequently noisy. If he looks to the right and
the left and sees old soldiers—men of twelve years'
service, who, he knows, know what they are about—
taking a charge, rush, or demonstration without
embarrassment, he is consoled and applies his
shoulder to the butt of his rifle with a stout heart.
His peace is the greater if he hears a senior, who
has taught him his soldiering and broken his head

on occasion, whispering : ' They'll shout and carry
on like this for five minutes. Then they'll rush in,
and then we've got 'em by the short hairs ! '

But, on the other hand, if he sees only men of
his own term of service, turning white and playing
with their triggers and saying : ' What the Hell's up
now ?' while the Company Commanders are sweating into their sword-hilts and shouting : ' Front-rank,
fix bayonets. Steady there—steady ! Sight for
three hundred—no, for five ! Lie down, all ! Steady !
Fronk-rank kneel !' and so forth, he becomes un-
happy ; and grows acutely miserable when he hears
a comrade turn over with the rattle of fire-irons
falling into the fender, and the grunt of a pole-axed
ox. If he can be moved about a little and allowed
to watch the effect of his own fire on the enemy
he feels merrier, and may be then worked up to
the blind passion of fighting, which is, contrary to
general belief, controlled by a chilly Devil and
shakes men like ague. If he is not moved about,
and begins to feel cold at the pit of the stomach,
and in that crisis is badly mauled and hears orders
that were never given, he will break, and he will
break badly ; and of all things under the light of
the Sun there is nothing more terrible than a broken
British regiment. When the worst comes to the
worst and the panic is really epidemic, the men
must be e'en let go, and the Company Commanders
had better escape to the enemy and stay there for
safety's sake. If they can be made to come again
they are not pleasant men to meet ; because they
will not break twice.

About thirty years from this date, when we have

succeeded in half-educating everything that wears
trousers, our Army will be a beautifully unreliable
machine.   It will know too much and it will do too
little.   Later still, when all men are at the mental
level of the officer of to-day, it will sweep the earth.
Speaking roughly, you must employ either blackguards or gentlemen, or, best of all, blackguards
commanded by gentlemen, to do butcher's work with
efficiency and despatch.   The ideal soldier should, of
course, think for himself—the *Pocket-book* says so.
Unfortunately, to attain this virtue he has to pass
through the phase of thinking of himself, and that is
misdirected genius.   A blackguard may be slow to
think for himself, but he is genuinely anxious to kill,
and a little punishment teaches him how to guard
his own skin and perforate another's.   A powerfully
prayerful Highland Regiment, officered by rank
Presbyterians, is, perhaps, one degree more terrible
in action than a hard-bitten thousand of irresponsible
Irish ruffians led by most improper young un-
believers.   But these things prove the rule—which is
that the midway men are not to be trusted alone.
They have ideas about the value of life and an up-
bringing that has not taught them to go on and
take the chances.   They are carefully unprovided with
a backing of comrades who have been shot over, and
until that backing is re-introduced, as a great many
Regimental Commanders intend it shall be, they are
more liable to disgrace themselves than the size of
the Empire or the dignity of the Army allows.
Their officers are as good as good can be, because
their training begins early, and God has arranged
that a clean-run youth of the British middle classes

shall, in the matter of backbone, brains, and bowels, surpass all other youths. For this reason a child of eighteen will stand up, doing nothing, with a tin sword in his hand and joy in his heart until he is dropped. If he dies, he dies like a gentleman. If he lives, he writes Home that he has been 'potted,' 'sniped,' 'chipped,' or 'cut over,' and sits down to besiege Government for a wound-gratuity until the next little war breaks out, when he perjures himself before a Medical Board, blarneys his Colonel, burns incense round his Adjutant, and is allowed to go to the Front once more.

Which homily brings me directly to a brace of the most finished little fiends that ever banged drum or tootled fife in the Band of a British Regiment. They ended their sinful career by open and flagrant mutiny and were shot for it. Their names were Jakin and Lew—Piggy Lew—and they were bold, bad drummer-boys, both of them frequently birched by the Drum-Major of the Fore and Aft.

Jakin was a stunted child of fourteen, and Lew was about the same age. When not looked after, they smoked and drank. They swore habitually after the manner of the Barrack-room, which is cold-swearing and comes from between clinched teeth; and they fought religiously once a week. Jakin had sprung from some London gutter, and may or may not have passed through Dr. Barnardo's hands ere he arrived at the dignity of drummer-boy. Lew could remember nothing except the regiment and the delight of listening to the Band from his earliest years. He hid somewhere in his grimy little soul a genuine love for music, and was most mistakenly

furnished with the head of a cherub : insomuch that
beautiful ladies who watched the Regiment in church
were wont to speak of him as a 'darling.'   They
never heard his vitriolic comments on their manners
and morals, as he walked back to barracks with the
Band and matured fresh causes of offence against
Jakin.

The other drummer-boys hated both lads on
account of their illogical conduct.   Jakin might be
pounding Lew, or Lew might be rubbing Jakin's
head in the dirt, but any attempt at aggression on
the part of an outsider was met by the combined
forces of Lew and Jakin ; and the consequences were
painful.   The boys were the Ishmaels of the corps,
but wealthy Ishmaels, for they sold battles in alternate
weeks for the sport of the barracks when they were
not pitted against other boys; and thus amassed
money.

On this particular day there was dissension in the
camp.   They had just been convicted afresh of
smoking, which is bad for little boys who use plug-
tobacco, and Lew's contention was that Jakin had
'stunk so 'orrid bad from keepin' the pipe in pocket,'
that he and he alone was responsible for the birching
they were both tingling under.

'I tell you I 'id the pipe back o' barracks,' said
Jakin pacifically.

'You're a bloomin' liar,' said Lew without heat.

'You're a bloomin' little barstard,' said Jakin,
strong in the knowledge that his own ancestry was
unknown.

Now there is one word in the extended vocabulary
of barrack-room abuse that cannot pass without com-

ment.   You may call a man a thief and risk nothing.
You may even call him a coward without finding more
than a boot whiz past your ear, but you must not
call a man a bastard unless you are prepared to
prove it on his front teeth.

'You might ha' kep' that till I wasn't so sore,'
said Lew sorrowfully, dodging round Jakin's guard.

'I'll make you sorer,' said Jakin genially, and got
home on Lew's alabaster forehead.   All would have
gone well and this story, as the books say, would
never have been written, had not his evil fate
prompted the Bazar-Sergeant's son, a long, employ-
less man of five-and-twenty, to put in an appearance
after the first round.   He was eternally in need of
money, and knew that the boys had silver.

'Fighting again,' said he.   'I'll report you to my
father, and he'll report you to the Colour-Sergeant.'

'What's that to you?' said Jakin with an unpleasant dilation of the nostrils.

'Oh! nothing to *me*.   You'll get into trouble,
and you've been up too often to afford that.'

'What the Hell do you know about what we've
done?' asked Lew the Seraph.   '*You* aren't in the
Army, you lousy, cadging civilian.'

He closed in on the man's left flank.

'Jes' 'cause you find two gentlemen settlin' their
diff'rences with their fistes you stick in your ugly
nose where you aren't wanted.   Run 'ome to your
'arf-caste slut of a Ma—or we'll give you what-for,'
said Jakin.

The man attempted reprisals by knocking the
boys' heads together.   The scheme would have succeeded had not Jakin punched him vehemently in the

'Hey! What? Are you going to argue with *me?*' said the Colonel.—P. 29.

stomach, or had Lew refrained from kicking his shins. They fought together, bleeding and breathless, for half an hour, and, after heavy punishment, triumphantly pulled down their opponent as terriers pull down a jackal.

'Now,' gasped Jakin, 'I'll give you what-for.' He proceeded to pound the man's features while Lew stamped on the outlying portions of his anatomy. Chivalry is not a strong point in the composition of the average drummer-boy. He fights, as do his betters, to make his mark.

Ghastly was the ruin that escaped, and awful was the wrath of the Bazar-Sergeant. Awful, too, was the scene in Orderly-room when the two reprobates appeared to answer the charge of half-murdering a 'civilian.' The Bazar-Sergeant thirsted for a criminal action, and his son lied. The boys stood to attention while the black clouds of evidence accumulated.

'You little devils are more trouble than the rest of the Regiment put together,' said the Colonel angrily. 'One might as well admonish thistledown, and I can't well put you in cells or under stoppages. You must be birched again.'

'Beg y' pardon, Sir. Can't we say nothin' in our own defence, Sir?' shrilled Jakin.

'Hey! What? Are you going to argue with *me*?' said the Colonel.

'No, Sir,' said Lew. 'But if a man come to you, Sir, and said he was going to report you, Sir, for 'aving a bit of a turn-up with a friend, Sir, an' wanted to get money out o' *you*, Sir——'

The Orderly-room exploded in a roar of laughter. 'Well?' said the Colonel.

'That was what that measly *jarnwar* there did, Sir, and 'e'd 'a' *done* it, Sir, if we 'adn't prevented 'im. We didn't 'it 'im much, Sir. 'E 'adn't no manner o' right to interfere with us, Sir. I don't mind bein' birched by the Drum-Major, Sir, nor yet reported by *any* Corp'ral, but I'm—but I don't think it's fair, Sir, for a civilian to come an' talk over a man in the Army.'

A second shout of laughter shook the Orderly-room, but the Colonel was grave.

'What sort of characters have these boys?' he asked of the Regimental Sergeant-Major.

'Accordin' to the Bandmaster, Sir,' returned that revered official—the only soul in the regiment whom the boys feared—'they do everything *but* lie, Sir.'

'Is it like we'd go for that man for fun, Sir?' said Lew, pointing to the plaintiff.

'Oh, admonished—admonished!' said the Colonel testily, and when the boys had gone he read the Bazar-Sergeant's son a lecture on the sin of unprofitable meddling, and gave orders that the Bandmaster should keep the Drums in better discipline.

'If either of you comes to practice again with so much as a scratch on your two ugly little faces,' thundered the Bandmaster, 'I'll tell the Drum-Major to take the skin off your backs. Understand that, you young devils.'

Then he repented of his speech for just the length of time that Lew, looking like a Seraph in red worsted embellishments, took the place of one of the trumpets—in hospital—and rendered the echo of a battle-piece. Lew certainly was a musician, and had often in his more exalted moments expressed a yearning to master every instrument of the Band.

'There's nothing to prevent your becoming a Bandmaster, Lew,' said the Bandmaster, who had composed waltzes of his own, and worked day and night in the interests of the Band.

'What did he say?' demanded Jakin after practice.

''Said I might be a bloomin' Bandmaster, an' be asked in to 'ave a glass o' sherry-wine on Mess-nights.'

'Ho! 'Said you might be a bloomin' non-com-batant, did 'e! That's just about wot 'e would say. When I've put in my boy's service—it's a bloomin' shame that doesn't count for pension—I'll take on as a privit. Then I'll be a Lance in a year—know-in' what I know about the ins an' outs o' things. In three years I'll be a bloomin' Sergeant. I won't marry then, not I! I'll 'old on and learn the orf'cers' ways an' apply for exchange into a reg'ment that doesn't know all about me. Then I'll be a bloomin' orf'cer. Then I'll ask you to 'ave a glass o' sherry-wine, *Mister* Lew, an' you'll bloomin' well 'ave to stay in the hanty-room while the Mess-Sergeant brings it to your dirty 'ands.'

''S'pose I'm going to be a Bandmaster? Not I, quite. I'll be a orf'cer too. There's nothin' like taking to a thing an' stickin' to it, the Schoolmaster says. The reg'ment don't go 'ome for another seven years. I'll be a Lance then or near to.'

Thus the boys discussed their futures, and con-ducted themselves piously for a week. That is to say, Lew started a flirtation with the Colour-Sergeant's daughter, aged thirteen—'not,' as he explained to Jakin, ' with any intention o' matrimony, but by way o' keepin' my 'and in.' And the black-haired Cris Delighan enjoyed that flirtation more than previous ones, and the other drummer-boys raged furiously together, and Jakin preached sermons on the dangers of 'bein' tangled along o' petticoats.'

But neither love nor virtue would have held Lew long in the paths of propriety had not the rumour gone abroad that the Regiment was to be sent on active service, to take part in a war which, for the sake of brevity, we will call 'The War of the Lost Tribes.'

The barracks had the rumour almost before the Mess-room, and of all the nine hundred men in barracks not ten had seen a shot fired in anger. The Colonel had, twenty years ago, assisted at a Frontier expedition ; one of the Majors had seen service at the Cape ; a confirmed deserter in E Company had helped to clear streets in Ireland ; but that was all. The Regiment had been put by for many years. The overwhelming mass of its rank and file had from three to four years' service ; the non-commissioned officers were under thirty years old ; and men and sergeants alike had forgotten to speak of the stories written in brief upon the Colours—the New Colours that had been formally blessed by an Archbishop in England ere the Regiment came away.

They wanted to go to the Front—they were enthusiastically anxious to go—but they had no knowledge of what war meant, and there was none to tell them. They were an educated regiment, the percentage of school-certificates in their ranks was high, and most of the men could do more than read and write. They had been recruited in loyal observance of the territorial idea ; but they themselves had no notion of that idea. They were made up of drafts from an over-populated manufacturing district. The system had put flesh and muscle upon their small bones, but it could not put heart into the sons of those who for generations had done overmuch work for over-scanty pay, had sweated in drying-rooms, stooped over looms, coughed among white-lead, and shivered on lime-barges. The men had found food and rest in the Army, and now they were going to fight ' niggers '—people who ran away if you shook a stick at them. Wherefore they cheered lustily when the rumour ran, and the shrewd, clerkly non-commissioned officers speculated on the chances of batta and of saving their pay. At Headquarters men said : ' The Fore and Fit have never been under fire within the last generation. Let us, therefore, break them in easily by setting them to guard lines of communication.' And this would have been done but for the fact that British Regiments were wanted—badly wanted—at the Front, and there were doubtful Native Regiments that could fill the minor duties. ' Brigade 'em with two strong Regiments,' said Headquarters. ' They may be knocked about a bit, but they'll learn their business before they come through. Nothing like a night-alarm and a little cutting up of stragglers to make a Regiment smart in the field. Wait till they've had half-a-dozen sentries' throats cut.'

The Colonel wrote with delight that the temper of his men was excellent, that the Regiment was all that could be wished and as sound as a bell. The

Majors smiled with a sober joy, and the subalterns
waltzed in pairs down the Mess-room after dinner,
and nearly shot themselves at revolver-practice. But
there was consternation in the hearts of Jakin and
Lew. What was to be done with the Drums?
Would the Band go to the Front? How many of
the Drums would accompany the Regiment?

They took counsel together, sitting in a tree and
smoking.

'It's more than a bloomin' toss-up they'll leave
us be'ind at the Depot with the women. You'll like
that,' said Jakin sarcastically.

''Cause o' Cris, y' mean? Wot's a woman, or a
'ole bloomin' depot o' women, 'longside o' the chanst
of field-service? You know I'm as keen on goin' as
you,' said Lew.

''Wish I was a bloomin' bugler,' said Jakin sadly.
'They'll take Tom Kidd along, that I can plaster a
wall with, an' like as not they won't take us.'

'Then let's go an' make Tom Kidd so bloomin'
sick 'e can't bugle no more. You 'old 'is 'ands an'
I'll kick him,' said Lew, wriggling on the branch.

'That ain't no good neither. We ain't the sort
o' characters to presoom on our rep'tations—they're
bad. If they leave the Band at the Depot we don't
go, and no error *there*. If they take the Band we
may get cast for medical unfitness. Are you
medical fit, Piggy?' said Jakin, digging Lew in the
ribs with force.

'Yus,' said Lew with an oath. 'The Doctor
says your 'eart's weak through smokin' on an empty
stummick. Throw a chest an' I'll try yer.'

Jakin threw out his chest, which Lew smote with

all his might. Jakin turned very pale, gasped,
crowed, screwed up his eyes, and said—'That's all
right.'

'You'll do,' said Lew. 'I've 'eard o' men dying
when you 'it 'em fair on the breastbone.'

'Don't bring us no nearer goin', though,' said
Jakin. 'Do you know where we're ordered?'

'Gawd knows, an' 'E won't split on a pal. Somewheres up to the Front to kill Paythans—hairy big
beggars that turn you inside out if they get 'old
o' you. They say their women are good-looking,
too.'

'Any loot?' asked the abandoned Jakin.

'Not a bloomin' anna, they say, unless you dig
up the ground an' see what the niggers 'ave 'id.
They're a poor lot.' Jakin stood upright on the
branch and gazed across the plain.

'Lew,' said he, 'there's the Colonel coming.
'Colonel's a good old beggar. Let's go an' talk to
'im.'

Lew nearly fell out of the tree at the audacity of
the suggestion. Like Jakin he feared not. God,
neither regarded he Man, but there are limits even
to the audacity of drummer-boy, and to speak to a
Colonel was——

But Jakin had slid down the trunk and doubled
in the direction of the Colonel. That officer was
walking wrapped in thought and visions of a C.B.—
yes, even a K.C.B., for had he not at command one
of the best Regiments of the Line—the Fore and
Fit? And he was aware of two small boys charging
down upon him. Once before it had been solemnly
reported to him that 'the Drums were in a state of

mutiny,' Jakin and Lew being the ringleaders. This looked like an organised conspiracy.

The boys halted at twenty yards, walked to the regulation four paces, and saluted together, each as well-set-up as a ramrod and little taller.

The Colonel was in a genial mood; the boys appeared very forlorn and unprotected on the desolate plain, and one of them was handsome.

'Well!' said the Colonel, recognising them. 'Are you going to pull me down in the open? I'm sure I never interfere with you, even though'—he sniffed suspiciously—'you have been smoking.'

It was time to strike while the iron was hot. Their hearts beat tumultuously.

'Beg y' pardon, Sir,' began Jakin. 'The Reg'ment's ordered on active service, Sir?'

'So I believe,' said the Colonel courteously.

'Is the Band goin', Sir?' said both together. Then, without pause, 'We're goin', Sir, ain't we?'

'You!' said the Colonel, stepping back the more fully to take in the two small figures. 'You! You'd die in the first march.'

'No, we wouldn't, Sir. We can march with the Reg'ment anywheres—p'rade an' anywhere else,' said Jakin.

'If Tom Kidd goes 'e'll shut up like a clasp-knife,' said Lew. 'Tom 'as very-close veins in both 'is legs, Sir.'

'Very how much?'

'Very-close veins, Sir. That's why they swells after long p'rade, Sir. If 'e can go, we can go, Sir.'

Again the Colonel looked at them long and intently.

'Yes, the Band is going,' he said as gravely as though he had been addressing a brother officer. 'Have you any parents, either of you two?'

'No, Sir,' rejoicingly from Lew and Jakin. 'We're both orphans, Sir. There's no one to be considered of on our account, Sir.'

'You poor little sprats, and you want to go up to the Front with the Regiment, do you? Why?'

'I've wore the Queen's Uniform for two years,' said Jakin. 'It's very 'ard, Sir, that a man don't get no recompense for doin' of 'is dooty, Sir.'

'An'—an' if I don't go, Sir,' interrupted Lew, 'the Bandmaster 'e says 'e'll catch an' make a bloo— a blessed musician o' me, Sir. Before I've seen any service, Sir.'

The Colonel made no answer for a long time. Then he said quietly : 'If you're passed by the Doctor I daresay you can go. I shouldn't smoke if I were you.'

The boys saluted and disappeared. The Colonel walked home and told the story to his wife, who nearly cried over it. The Colonel was well pleased. If that was the temper of the children, what would not the men do?

Jakin and Lew entered the boys' barrack-room with great stateliness, and refused to hold any conversation with their comrades for at least ten minutes. Then, bursting with pride, Jakin drawled : 'I've bin intervooin' the Colonel. Good old beggar is the Colonel. Says I to 'im, "Colonel," says I, "let me go to the Front, along o' the Reg'ment."—"To the Front you shall go," says 'e, "an' I only wish there was more like you among the dirty little devils that bang the bloomin' drums." Kidd, if you throw your 'courtrements at me for tellin' you the truth to your own advantage, your legs 'll swell.'

None the less there was a Battle-Royal in the barrack-room, for the boys were consumed with envy and hate, and neither Jakin nor Lew behaved in conciliatory wise.

' I'm goin' out to say adoo to my girl,' said Lew, to cap the climax. ' Don't none o' you touch my kit because it's wanted for active service; me bein' specially invited to go by the Colonel.'

He strolled forth and whistled in the clump of trees at the back of the Married Quarters till Cris came to him, and, the preliminary kisses being given and taken, Lew began to explain the situation.

' I'm goin' to the Front with the Reg'ment,' he said valiantly.

' Piggy, you're a little liar,' said Cris, but her heart misgave her, for Lew was not in the habit of lying.

' Liar yourself, Cris,' said Lew, slipping an arm round her. ' I'm goin'. When the Reg'ment marches out you'll see me with 'em, all galliant and gay. Give us another kiss, Cris, on the strength of it.'

' If you'd on'y a-stayed at the Depot—where you *ought* to ha' bin—you could get as many of 'em as —as you dam please,' whimpered Cris, putting up her mouth.

' It's 'ard, Cris. I grant you it's 'ard. But what's a man to do? If I'd a-stayed at the Depot, you wouldn't think anything of me.'

' Like as not, but I'd 'ave you with me, Piggy. An' all the thinkin' in the world isn't like kissin'.'

Cris slid an arm round his neck. —P. 39.

' An' all the kissin' in the world isn't like 'avin' a medal to wear on the front o' your coat.'

' *You* won't get no medal.'

' Oh yus, I shall though.   Me an' Jakin arc the only acting-drummers that'll be took along.   All. the rest is full men, an' we'll get our medals with them.'

' They might ha' taken anybody but you, Piggy. You'll get killed — you're so venturesome.   Stay with me, Piggy darlin', down at the Depot, an' I'll love you true for ever.'

' Ain't you goin' to do that *now*, Cris ?   You said you was.'

' O' course I am, but th' other's more comfortable. Wait till you've growed a bit, Piggy.   You aren't no taller than me now.'

' I've bin in the Army for two years an' I'm not goin' to get out of a chanst o' seein' service, an' don't you try to make me do so.   I'll come back, Cris, an' when I take on as a man I'll marry you—marry you when I'm a Lance.'

' Promise, Piggy ! '

Lew reflected on the future as arranged by Jakin a short time previously, but Cris's mouth was very near to his own.

' I promise, s'elp me Gawd ! ' said he.

Cris slid an arm round his neck.

' I won't 'old you back no more, Piggy.   Go away an' get your medal, an' I'll make you a new button-bag as nice as I know how,' she whispered.

' Put some o' your 'air into it, Cris, an' I'll keep it in my pocket so long's I'm alive.'

Then Cris wept anew, and the interview ended.

Public feeling among the drummer - boys rose to fever pitch and the lives of Jakin and Lew became unenviable. Not only had they been permitted to enlist two years before the regulation boy's age—fourteen—but, by virtue, it seemed, of their extreme youth, they were allowed to go to the Front—which thing had not happened to acting-drummers within the knowledge of boy. The Band which was to accompany the Regiment had been cut down to the regulation twenty men, the surplus returning to the ranks. Jakin and Lew were attached to the Band as supernumeraries, though they would much have preferred being Company buglers.

''Don't matter much,' said Jakin after the medical inspection. 'Be thankful that we're 'lowed to go at all. The Doctor 'e said that if we could stand what we took from the Bazar-Sergeant's son we'd stand pretty nigh anything.'

'Which we will,' said Lew, looking tenderly at the ragged and ill-made housewife that Cris had given him, with a lock of her hair worked into a sprawling 'L' upon the cover.

'It was the best I could,' she sobbed. 'I wouldn't let mother nor the Sergeants' tailor 'elp me. Keep it always, Piggy, an' remember I love you true.'

They marched to the railway station, nine hundred and sixty strong, and every soul in cantonments turned out to see them go. The drummers gnashed their teeth at Jakin and Lew marching with the Band, the married women wept upon the platform, and the Regiment cheered its noble self black in the face.

'A nice level lot,' said the Colonel to the Second-in-Command as they watched the first four companies entraining.

'Fit to do anything,' said the Second-in-Command enthusiastically. 'But it seems to me they're a thought too young and tender for the work in hand. It's bitter cold up at the Front now.'

'They're sound enough,' said the Colonel. 'We must take our chance of sick casualties.'

So they went northward, ever northward, past droves and droves of camels, armies of camp followers, and legions of laden mules, the throng thickening day by day, till with a shriek the train pulled up at a hopelessly-congested junction where six lines of temporary track accommodated six forty-waggon trains; where whistles blew, Babus sweated, and Commissariat officers swore from dawn till far into the night amid the wind-driven chaff of the fodder-bales and the lowing of a thousand steers.

'Hurry up—you're badly wanted at the Front,' was the message that greeted the Fore and Aft, and the occupants of the Red Cross carriages told the same tale.

''Tisn't so much the bloomin' fightin',' gasped a headbound trooper of Hussars to a knot of admiring Fore and Afts. ''Tisn't so much the bloomin' fightin', though there's enough o' that. It's the bloomin' food an' the bloomin' climate. Frost all night 'cept when it hails, and biling sun all day, and the water stinks fit to knock you down. I got my 'ead chipped like a egg; I've got pneumonia too, an' my guts is all out o' order. 'Tain't no bloomin' picnic in those parts, I can tell you.'

'Wot are the niggers like?' demanded a private.

'There's some prisoners in that train yonder. Go an' look at 'em. They're the aristocracy o' the country. The common folk are a dashed sight uglier. If you want to know what they fight with, reach under my seat an' pull out the long knife that's there.'

They dragged out and beheld for the first time the grim, bone-handled, triangular Afghan knife. It was almost as long as Lew.

'That's the thing to jint ye,' said the trooper feebly. 'It can take off a man's arm at the shoulder as easy as slicing butter. I halved the beggar that used that 'un, but there's more of his likes up above. They don't understand thrustin', but they're devils to slice.'

The men strolled across the tracks to inspect the Afghan prisoners. They were unlike any 'niggers' that the Fore and Aft had ever met—these huge, black-haired, scowling sons of the Beni-Israel. As the men stared the Afghans spat freely and muttered one to another with lowered eyes.

'My eyes! Wot awful swine!' said Jakin, who was in the rear of the procession. 'Say, old man, how you got *puckrowed*, eh? *Kiswasti* you wasn't hanged for your ugly face, hey?'

The tallest of the company turned, his leg-irons clanking at the movement, and stared at the boy. 'See!' he cried to his fellows in Pushto. 'They send children against us. What a people, and what fools!'

'*Hya!*' said Jakin, nodding his head cheerily. 'You go down-country. *Khana* get, *peenikapanee* get—live like a bloomin' Raja *ke marfik*. That's a

The men strolled across the tracks to inspect the Afghan prisoners. —P. 42.

better *bandobust* than baynit get it in your innards.
Good-bye, ole man. Take care o' your beautiful
figure-'ed, an' try to look *kushy*.'

The men laughed and fell in for their first march,
when they began to realise that a soldier's life was
not all beer and skittles. They were much impressed
with the size and bestial ferocity of the niggers whom
they had now learned to call 'Paythans,' and more
with the exceeding discomfort of their own sur-
roundings. Twenty old soldiers in the corps would
have taught them how to make themselves moderately
snug at night, but they had no old soldiers, and, as
the troops on the line of march said, 'they lived like
pigs.' They learned the heart-breaking cussedness
of camp-kitchens and camels and the depravity of
an E. P. tent and a wither-wrung mule. They
studied animalculæ in water, and developed a few
cases of dysentery in their study.

At the end of their third march they were dis-
agreeably surprised by the arrival in their camp of
a hammered iron slug which, fired from a steady rest
at seven hundred yards, flicked out the brains of a
private seated by the fire. This robbed them of
their peace for a night, and was the beginning of a
long-range fire carefully calculated to that end. In
the daytime they saw nothing except an unpleasant
puff of smoke from a crag above the line of march.
At night there were distant spurts of flame and
occasional casualties, which set the whole camp
blazing into the gloom and, occasionally, into
opposite tents. Then they swore vehemently and
vowed that this was magnificent, but not war.

Indeed it was not. The Regiment could not halt

for reprisals against the sharpshooters of the countryside. Its duty was to go forward and make con-
nection with the Scotch and Gurkha troops with
which it was brigaded. The Afghans knew this,
and knew too, after their first tentative shots, that
they were dealing with a raw regiment. Thereafter
they devoted themselves to the task of keeping the
Fore and Aft on the strain. Not for anything would
they have taken equal liberties with a seasoned corps
—with the wicked little Gurkhas, whose delight it
was to lie out in the open on a dark night and stalk
their stalkers—with the terrible, big men dressed in
women's clothes, who could be heard praying to
their God in the night-watches, and whose peace of
mind no amount of 'sniping' could shake—or with
those vile Sikhs, who marched so ostentatiously un-
prepared and who dealt out such grim reward to
those who tried to profit by that unpreparedness.
This white regiment was different—quite different.
It slept like a hog, and, like a hog, charged in every
direction when it was roused. Its sentries walked
with a footfall that could be heard for a quarter of a
mile ; would fire at anything that moved—even a
driven donkey—and when they had once fired, could
be scientifically 'rushed' and laid out a horror and
an offence against the morning sun. Then there
were camp-followers who straggled and could be cut
up without fear. Their shrieks would disturb the
white boys, and the loss of their services would in-
convenience them sorely.

Thus, at every march, the hidden enemy became
bolder and the regiment writhed and twisted under
attacks it could not avenge. The crowning triumph

was a sudden night-rush ending in the cutting of many tent-ropes, the collapse of the sodden canvas, and a glorious knifing of the men who struggled and kicked below. It was a great deed, neatly carried out, and it shook the already shaken nerves of the Fore and Aft. All the courage that they had been required to exercise up to this point was the 'two o'clock in the morning courage'; and, so far, they had only succeeded in shooting their comrades and losing their sleep.

Sullen, discontented, cold, savage, sick, with their uniforms dulled and unclean, the Fore and Aft joined their Brigade.

'I hear you had a tough time of it coming up,' said the Brigadier. But when he saw the hospital-sheets his face fell.

'This is bad,' said he to himself. 'They're as rotten as sheep.' And aloud to the Colonel—'I'm afraid we can't spare you just yet. We want all we have, else I should have given you ten days to recover in.'

The Colonel winced. 'On my honour, Sir,' he returned, 'there is not the least necessity to think of sparing us. My men have been rather mauled and upset without a fair return. They only want to go in somewhere where they can see what's before them.'

'Can't say I think much of the Fore and Fit,' said the Brigadier in confidence to his Brigade-Major. 'They've lost all their soldiering, and, by the trim of them, might have marched through the country from the other side. A more fagged-out set of men I never put eyes on.'

'Oh, they'll improve as the work goes on. The parade gloss has been rubbed off a little, but they'll put on field polish before long,' said the Brigade-Major. 'They've been mauled, and they don't quite understand it.'

They did not. All the hitting was on one side, and it was cruelly hard hitting with accessories that made them sick. There was also the real sickness that laid hold of a strong man and dragged him howling to the grave. Worst of all, their officers knew just as little of the country as the men themselves, and looked as if they did. The Fore and Aft were in a thoroughly unsatisfactory condition, but they believed that all would be well if they could once get a fair go-in at the enemy. Pot-shots up and down the valleys were unsatisfactory, and the bayonet never seemed to get a chance. Perhaps it was as well, for a long-limbed Afghan with a knife had a reach of eight feet, and could carry away lead that would disable three Englishmen.

The Fore and Fit would like some rifle-practice at the enemy—all seven hundred rifles blazing together. That wish showed the mood of the men.

The Gurkhas walked into their camp, and in broken, barrack-room English strove to fraternise with them; offered them pipes of tobacco and stood them treat at the canteen. But the Fore and Aft, not knowing much of the nature of the Gurkhas, treated them as they would treat any other 'niggers,' and the little men in green trotted back to their firm friends the Highlanders, and with many grins confided to them: 'That dam white regiment no dam use. Sulky—ugh! Dirty—ugh! Hya, any tot for Johnny?' Whereat the Highlanders smote the Gurkhas as to the head, and told them not to vilify a British Regiment, and the Gurkhas grinned cavernously, for the Highlanders were their elder brothers and entitled to the privileges of kinship. The common soldier who touches a Gurkha is more than likely to have his head sliced open.

Three days later the Brigadier arranged a battle according to the rules of war and the peculiarity of the Afghan temperament. The enemy were massing in inconvenient strength among the hills, and the moving of many green standards warned him that the tribes were 'up' in aid of the Afghan regular troops. A squadron and a half of Bengal Lancers represented the available Cavalry, and two screw-guns borrowed from a column thirty miles away the Artillery at the General's disposal.

'If they stand, as I've a very strong notion that they will, I fancy we shall see an infantry fight that will be worth watching,' said the Brigadier. 'We'll do it in style. Each regiment shall be played into action by its Band, and we'll hold the Cavalry in reserve.'

'For *all* the reserve?' somebody asked.

'For all the reserve; because we're going to crumple them up,' said the Brigadier, who was an extraordinary Brigadier, and did not believe in the value of a reserve when dealing with Asiatics. Indeed, when you come to think of it, had the British Army consistently waited for reserves in all its little affairs, the boundaries of Our Empire would have stopped at Brighton beach.

That battle was to be a glorious battle.

The three regiments debouching from three separate gorges, after duly crowning the heights above, were to converge from the centre, left, and right upon what we will call the Afghan army, then stationed towards the lower extremity of a flat-bottomed valley. Thus it will be seen that three sides of the valley practically belonged to the English, while the fourth was strictly Afghan property. In the event of defeat the Afghans had the rocky hills to fly to, where the fire from the guerilla tribes in aid would cover their retreat. In the event of victory these same tribes would rush down and lend their weight to the rout of the British.

The screw-guns were to shell the head of each Afghan rush that was made in close formation, and the Cavalry, held in reserve in the right valley, were to gently stimulate the break-up which would follow on the combined attack. The Brigadier, sitting upon a rock overlooking the valley, would watch the battle unrolled at his feet. The Fore and Aft would debouch from the central gorge, the Gurkhas from the left, and the Highlanders from the right, for the reason that the left flank of the enemy seemed as though it required the most hammering. It was not every day that an Afghan force would take ground in the open, and the Brigadier was resolved to make the most of it.

'If we only had a few more men,' he said plaintively, 'we could surround the creatures and crumple 'em up thoroughly. As it is, I'm afraid we can only cut them up as they run. It's a great pity.'

The Fore and Aft had enjoyed unbroken peace for five days, and were beginning, in spite of dysentery, to recover their nerve. But they were not happy, for they did not know the work in hand, and had they known, would not have known how to do it. Throughout those five days in which old soldiers might have taught them the craft of the game, they discussed together their misadventures in the past—how such an one was alive at dawn and dead ere the dusk, and with what shrieks and struggles such another had given up his soul under the Afghan knife. Death was a new and horrible thing to the sons of mechanics who were used to die decently of zymotic disease ; and their careful conservation in barracks had done nothing to make them look upon it with less dread.

Very early in the dawn the bugles began to blow, and the Fore and Aft, filled with a misguided enthusiasm, turned out without waiting for a cup of coffee and a biscuit ; and were rewarded by being kept under arms in the cold while the other regiments leisurely prepared for the fray. All the world knows that it is ill taking the breeks off a Highlander. It is much iller to try to make him stir unless he is convinced of the necessity for haste.

The Fore and Aft waited, leaning upon their rifles and listening to the protests of their empty stomachs. The Colonel did his best to remedy the default of lining as soon as it was borne in upon him that the affair would not begin at once, and so well did he succeed that the coffee was just ready when—the men moved off, their Band leading. Even then there had been a mistake in time, and the Fore and Aft came out into the valley ten minutes before the proper hour. Their Band wheeled

E

to the right after reaching the open, and retired behind a little rocky knoll still playing while the regiment went past.

It was not a pleasant sight that opened on the uninstructed view, for the lower end of the valley appeared to be filled by an army in position—real and actual regiments attired in red coats, and—of this there was no doubt—firing Martini-Henry bullets which cut up the ground a hundred yards in front of the leading company. Over that pock-marked ground the regiment had to pass, and it opened the ball with a general and profound courtesy to the piping pickets; ducking in perfect time, as though it had been brazed on a rod. Being half-capable of thinking for itself, it fired a volley by the simple process of pitching its rifle into its shoulder and pulling the trigger. The bullets may have accounted for some of the watchers on the hillside, but they certainly did not affect the mass of enemy in front, while the noise of the rifles drowned any orders that might have been given.

'Good God!' said the Brigadier, sitting on the rock high above all. 'That regiment has spoilt the whole show. Hurry up the others, and let the screw-guns get off.'

But the screw-guns, in working round the heights, had stumbled upon a wasp's nest of a small mud fort which they incontinently shelled at eight hundred yards, to the huge discomfort of the occupants, who were unaccustomed to weapons of such devilish precision.

The Fore and Aft continued to go forward, but with shortened stride. Where were the other regi-

ments, and why did these niggers use Martinis?
They took open order instinctively, lying down and
firing at random, rushing a few paces forward and
lying down again, according to the regulations.
Once in this formation, each man felt himself
desperately alone, and edged in towards his fellow
for comfort's sake.

Then the crack of his neighbour's rifle at his ear
led him to fire as rapidly as he could—again for the
sake of the comfort of the noise. The reward was
not long delayed. Five volleys plunged the files in
banked smoke impenetrable to the eye, and the
bullets began to take ground twenty or thirty yards
in front of the firers, as the weight of the bayonet
dragged down and to the right arms wearied with
holding the kick of the leaping Martini. The Company Commanders peered helplessly through the
smoke, the more nervous mechanically trying to fan
it away with their helmets.

'High and to the left!' bawled a Captain till he
was hoarse. 'No good! Cease firing, and let it
drift away a bit.'

Three and four times the bugles shrieked the
order, and when it was obeyed the Fore and Aft
looked that their foe should be lying before them in
mown swaths of men. A light wind drove the
smoke to leeward, and showed the enemy still in
position and apparently unaffected. A quarter of a
ton of lead had been buried a furlong in front of
them, as the ragged earth attested.

That was not demoralising to the Afghans, who
have not European nerves. They were waiting for
the mad riot to die down, and were firing quietly into

the heart of the smoke. A private of the Fore and Aft spun up his company shrieking with agony, another was kicking the earth and gasping, and a third, ripped through the lower intestines by a jagged bullet, was calling aloud on his comrades to put him out of his pain. These were the casualties, and they were not soothing to hear or see. The smoke cleared to a dull haze.

Then the foe began to shout with a great shouting, and a mass—a black mass—detached itself from the main body, and rolled over the ground at horrid speed. It was composed of, perhaps, three hundred men, who would shout and fire and slash if the rush of their fifty comrades who were determined to die carried home. The fifty were Ghazis, half-maddened with drugs and wholly mad with religious fanaticism. When they rushed the British fire ceased, and in the lull the order was given to close ranks and meet them with the bayonet.

Any one who knew the business could have told the Fore and Aft that the only way of dealing with a Ghazi rush is by volleys at long ranges ; because a man who means to die, who desires to die, who will gain heaven by dying, must, in nine cases out of ten, kill a man who has a lingering prejudice in favour of life. Where they should have closed and gone forward, the Fore and Aft opened out and skirmished, and where they should have opened out and fired, they closed and waited.

A man dragged from his blankets half awake and unfed is never in a pleasant frame of mind. Nor does his happiness increase when he watches the whites of the eyes of three hundred six-foot fiends upon whose beards the foam is lying, upon whose tongues is a roar of wrath, and in whose hands are yard-long knives.

The Fore and Aft heard the Gurkha bugles bringing that regiment forward at the double, while the neighing of the Highland pipes came from the left. They strove to stay where they were, though the bayonets wavered down the line like the oars of a ragged boat. Then they felt body to body the amazing physical strength of their foes; a shriek of pain ended the rush, and the knives fell amid scenes not to be told. The men clubbed together and smote blindly—as often as not at their own fellows. Their front crumpled like paper, and the fifty Ghazis passed on; their backers, now drunk with success, fighting as madly as they.

Then the rear-ranks were bidden to close up, and the subalterns dashed into the stew—alone. For the rear-rank had heard the clamour in front, the yells and the howls of pain, and had seen the dark stale blood that makes afraid. They were not going to stay. It was the rushing of the camps over again. Let their officers go to Hell, if they chose; they would get away from the knives.

'Come on!' shrieked the subalterns, and their men, cursing them, drew back, each closing into his neighbour and wheeling round.

Charteris and Devlin, subalterns of the last company, faced their death alone in the belief that their men would follow.

'You've killed me, you cowards,' sobbed Devlin and dropped, cut from the shoulder-strap to the centre of the chest, and a fresh detachment of his men retreating, always retreating, trampled him under foot as they made for the pass whence they had emerged.

> I kissed her in the kitchen and I kissed her in the hall.
>   Child'un, child'un, follow me !
> Oh Golly, said the cook, is he gwine to kiss us all ?
>   Halla—Halla—Halla—Hallelujah !

The Gurkhas were pouring through the left gorge and over the heights at the double to the invitation of their Regimental Quick-step. The black rocks were crowned with dark green spiders as the bugles gave tongue jubilantly :—

> In the morning ! In the morning *by* the bright light !
> When Gabriel blows his trumpet in the morning !

The Gurkha rear-companies tripped and blundered over loose stones. The front-files halted for a moment to take stock of the valley and to settle stray boot-laces. Then a happy little sigh of contentment soughed down the ranks, and it was as though the land smiled, for behold there below was the enemy, and it was to meet them that the Gurkhas had doubled so hastily. There was much enemy. There would be amusement. The little men hitched their *kukris* well to hand, and gaped expectantly at their officers as terriers grin ere the stone is cast for them to fetch. The Gurkhas' ground sloped downward to the valley, and they enjoyed a fair view of the proceedings. They sat upon the boulders to watch, for their officers were not going to waste their wind in assisting to repulse a Ghazi rush more than

half a mile away.   Let the white men look to their
own front.

'Hi! yi!' said the Subadar-Major, who was
sweating profusely.   'Dam fools yonder, stand close-
order!   This is no time for close order, it is the time
for volleys.   Ugh!'

Horrified, amused, and indignant, the Gurkhas
beheld the retirement of the Fore and Aft with a
running chorus of oaths and commentaries.

'They run!   The white men run!   Colonel Sahib,
may *we* also do a little running?' murmured Runbir
Thappa, the Senior Jemadar.

But the Colonel would have none of it.   'Let
the beggars be cut up a little,' said he wrath-
fully.   ''Serves 'em right.   They'll be prodded into
facing round in a minute.'   He looked through
his field-glasses, and caught the glint of an officer's
sword.

'Beating 'em with the flat—damned conscripts!
How the Ghazis are walking into them!' said he.

The Fore and Aft, heading back, bore with them
their officers.   The narrowness of the pass forced the
mob into solid formation, and the rear-rank delivered
some sort of a wavering volley.,   The Ghazis drew
off, for they did not know what reserves the gorge
might hide.   Moreover, it was never wise to chase
white men too far.   They returned as wolves return
to cover, satisfied with the slaughter that they had
done, and only stopping to slash at the wounded on
the ground.   A quarter of a mile had the Fore and
Aft retreated, and now, jammed in the pass, was
quivering with pain, shaken and demoralised with
fear, while the officers, maddened beyond control,

smote the men with the hilts and the flats of their swords.

'Get back! Get back, you cowards—you women! Right about face—column of companies, form—you hounds!' shouted the Colonel, and the subalterns swore aloud. But the Regiment wanted to go—to go anywhere out of the range of those merciless knives. It swayed to and fro irresolutely with shouts and outcries, while from the right the Gurkhas dropped volley after volley of cripple-stopper Snider bullets at long range into the mob of the Ghazis returning to their own troops.

The Fore and Aft Band, though protected from direct fire by the rocky knoll under which it had sat down, fled at the first rush. Jakin and Lew would have fled also, but their short legs left them fifty yards in the rear, and by the time the Band had mixed with the regiment, they were painfully aware that they would have to close in alone and unsupported.

'Get back to that rock,' gasped Jakin. 'They won't see us there.'

And they returned to the scattered instruments of the Band; their hearts nearly bursting their ribs.

'Here's a nice show for *us*,' said Jakin, throwing himself full length on the ground. 'A bloomin' fine show for British Infantry! Oh, the devils! They've gone an' left us alone here! Wot'll we do?'

Lew took possession of a cast-off water bottle, which naturally was full of canteen rum, and drank till he coughed again.

'Drink,' said he shortly.   'They'll come back in
a minute or two—you see.'

Jakin drank, but there was no sign of the
regiment's return.   They could hear a dull clamour
from the head of the valley of retreat, and saw the
Ghazis slink back, quickening their pace as the
Gurkhas fired at them.

'We're all that's left of the Band, an' we'll be cut
up as sure as death,' said Jakin.

'I'll die game, then,' said Lew thickly, fumbling
with his tiny drummer's sword.   The drink was
working on his brain as it was on Jakin's.

''Old on !   I know something better than fightin','
said Jakin, 'stung by the splendour of a sudden
thought' due chiefly to rum.   'Tip our bloomin'
cowards yonder the word to come back.   The
Paythan beggars are well away.   Come on, Lew !
We won't get hurt.   Take the fife an' give me the
drum.   The Old Step for all your bloomin' guts are
worth !   There's a few of our men coming back
now.   Stand up, ye drunken little defaulter.   By
your right—quick march !'

He slipped the drum - sling over his shoulder,
thrust the fife into Lew's hand, and the two boys
marched out of the cover of the rock into the open,
making a hideous hash of the first bars of the
' British Grenadiers.'

As Jakin had said, a few of the Fore and Aft were
coming back sullenly and shamefacedly under the
stimulus of blows and abuse ;   their red coats shone
at the head of the valley, and behind them were
wavering bayonets.   But between this shattered line
and the enemy, who with Afghan suspicion feared

that the hasty retreat meant an ambush, and had
not moved therefore, lay half a mile of level ground
dotted only by the wounded.

The tune settled into full swing and the boys
kept shoulder to shoulder, Jakin banging the drum
as one possessed. The one fife made a thin and
pitiful squeaking, but the tune carried far, even to
the Gurkhas.

'Come on, you dogs!' muttered Jakin to himself.
'Are we to play forhever?' Lew was staring straight
in front of him and marching more stiffly than ever
he had done on parade.

And in bitter mockery of the distant mob, the
old tune of the Old Line shrilled and rattled :—

> Some talk of Alexander,
>   And some of Hercules ;
> Of Hector and Lysander,
>   And such great names as these !

There was a far-off clapping of hands from the
Gurkhas, and a roar from the Highlanders in the
distance, but never a shot was fired by British or
Afghan. The two little red dots moved forward in
the open parallel to the enemy's front.

> But of all the world's great heroes
>   There's none that can compare,
> With a tow-row-row-row-row-row,
>   To the British Grenadier !

The men of the Fore and Aft were gathering
thick at the entrance to the plain. The Brigadier
on the heights far above was speechless with rage.
Still no movement from the enemy. The day stayed
to watch the children.

The tune settled into full swing and the boys kept shoulder to shoulder. —P. 58.

Jakin halted and beat the long roll of the Assembly, while the fife squealed despairingly.

'Right about face! Hold up, Lew, you're drunk,' said Jakin. They wheeled and marched back :—

> Those heroes of antiquity
> Ne'er saw a cannon-ball,
> Nor knew the force o' powder,

'Here they come!' said Jakin. 'Go on, Lew':—

> To scare their foes withal!

The Fore and Aft were pouring out of the valley. What officers had said to men in that time of shame and humiliation will never be known ; for neither officers nor men speak of it now.

'They are coming anew!' shouted a priest among the Afghans. 'Do not kill the boys! Take them alive, and they shall be of our faith.'

But the first volley had been fired, and Lew dropped on his face. Jakin stood for a minute, spun round and collapsed, as the Fore and Aft came forward, the curses of their officers in their ears, and in their hearts the shame of open shame.

Half the men had seen the drummers die, and they made no sign. They did not even shout. They doubled out straight across the plain in open order, and they did not fire.

'This,' said the Colonel of Gurkhas softly, 'is the real attack, as it should have been delivered. Come on, my children.'

'Ulu-lu-lu-lu!' squealed the Gurkhas, and came down with a joyful clicking of *kukris*—those vicious Gurkha knives.

On the right there was no rush. The Highlanders, cannily commending their souls to God (for it matters as much to a dead man whether he has been shot in a Border scuffle or at Waterloo), opened out and fired according to their custom, that is to say without heat and without intervals, while the screw-guns, having disposed of the impertinent mud fort aforementioned, dropped shell after shell into the clusters round the flickering green standards on the heights.

'Charrging is an unfortunate necessity,' murmured the Colour-Sergeant of the right company of the Highlanders. 'It makes the men sweer so, but I am thinkin' that it will come to a charrge if these black devils stand much longer. Stewarrt, man, you're firing into the eye of the sun, and he'll not take any harm for Government ammuncetion. A foot lower and a great deal slower! What are the English doing? They're very quiet there in the centre. Running again?'

The English were not running. They were hacking and hewing and stabbing, for though one white man is seldom physically a match for an Afghan in a sheepskin or wadded coat, yet, through the pressure of many white men behind, and a certain thirst for revenge in his heart, he becomes capable of doing much with both ends of his rifle. The Fore and Aft held their fire till one bullet could drive through five or six men, and the front of the Afghan force gave on the volley. They then selected their men, and slew them with deep gasps and short hacking coughs, and groanings of leather belts against strained bodies, and realised for the first time that an Afghan attacked is far less formidable than an

Afghan attacking: which fact old soldiers might have told them.

But they had no old soldiers in their ranks.

The Gurkhas' stall at the bazar was the noisiest, for the men were engaged—to a nasty noise as of beef being cut on the block—with the *kukri*, which they preferred to the bayonet; well knowing how the Afghan hates the half-moon blade.

As the Afghans wavered, the green standards on the mountain moved down to assist them in a last rally. This was unwise. The Lancers chafing in the right gorge had thrice despatched their only subaltern as galloper to report on the progress of affairs. On the third occasion he returned, with a bullet-graze on his knee, swearing strange oaths in Hindustani, and saying that all things were ready. So that Squadron swung round the right of the Highlanders with a wicked whistling of wind in the pennons of its lances, and fell upon the remnant just when, according to all the rules of war, it should have waited for the foe to show more signs of wavering.

But it was a dainty charge, deftly delivered, and it ended by the Cavalry finding itself at the head of the pass by which the Afghans intended to retreat; and down the track that the lances had made streamed two companies of the Highlanders, which was never intended by the Brigadier. The new development was successful. It detached the enemy from his base as a sponge is torn from a rock, and left him ringed about with fire in that pitiless plain. And as a sponge is chased round the bath-tub by the hand of the bather, so were the Afghans chased till they broke into little detachments much more difficult to dispose of than large masses.

'See!' quoth the Brigadier. 'Everything has come as I arranged. We've cut their base, and now we'll bucket 'em to pieces.'

A direct hammering was all that the Brigadier had dared to hope for, considering the size of the force at his disposal; but men who stand or fall by the errors of their opponents may be forgiven for turning Chance into Design. The bucketing went forward merrily. The Afghan forces were upon the run—the run of wearied wolves who snarl and bite over their shoulders. The red lances dipped by twos and threes, and, with a shriek, up rose the lance-butt, like a spar on a stormy sea, as the trooper cantering forward cleared his point. The Lancers kept between their prey and the steep hills, for all who could were trying to escape from the valley of death. The Highlanders gave the fugitives two hundred yards' law, and then brought them down, gasping and choking ere they could reach the protection of the boulders above. The Gurkhas followed suit; but the Fore and Aft were killing on their own account, for they had penned a mass of men between their bayonets and a wall of rock, and the flash of the rifles was lighting the wadded coats.

'We cannot hold them, Captain Sahib!' panted a Ressaidar of Lancers. 'Let us try the carbine. The lance is good, but it wastes time.'

They tried the carbine, and still the enemy melted away—fled up the hills by hundreds when there were only twenty bullets to stop them. On the heights the screw-guns ceased firing—they had run

out of ammunition—and the Brigadier groaned, for
the musketry fire could not sufficiently smash the
retreat.   Long before the last volleys were fired, the
doolies were out in force looking for the wounded.
The battle was over, and, but for want of fresh
troops, the Afghans would have been wiped off the
earth.   As it was they counted their dead by hundreds, and nowhere were the dead thicker than in
the track of the Fore and Aft.

But the Regiment did not cheer with the Highlanders, nor did they dance uncouth dances with the
Gurkhas among the dead.   They looked under their
brows at the Colonel as they leaned upon their rifles
and panted.

'Get back to camp, you.   Haven't you disgraced
yourself enough for one day !   Go and look to the
wounded.   It's all you're fit for,' said the Colonel.
Yet for the past hour the Fore and Aft had been
doing all that mortal commander could expect.
They had lost heavily because they did not know
how to set about their business with proper skill, but
they had borne themselves gallantly, and this was
their reward.

A young and sprightly Colour-Sergeant, who had
begun to imagine himself a hero, offered his water-
bottle to a Highlander, whose tongue was black with
thirst.   'I drink with no cowards,' answered the
youngster huskily, and, turning to a Gurkha, said,
'Hya, Johnny !   Drink water got it ?'   The Gurkha
grinned and passed his bottle.   The Fore and Aft
said no word.

They went back to camp when the field of strife
had been a little mopped up and made presentable,

and the Brigadier, who saw himself a Knight in three months, was the only soul who was complimentary to them. The Colonel was heart-broken, and the officers were savage and sullen.

'Well,' said the Brigadier, 'they are young troops of course, and it was not unnatural that they should retire in disorder for a bit.'

'Oh, my only Aunt Maria!' murmured a junior Staff Officer. 'Retire in disorder! It was a bally run!'

'But they came again, as we all know,' cooed the Brigadier, the Colonel's ashy-white face before him, 'and they behaved as well as could possibly be expected. Behaved beautifully, indeed. I was watching them. It's not a matter to take to heart, Colonel. As some German General said of his men, they wanted to be shooted over a little, that was all.' To himself he said—'Now they're blooded I can give 'em responsible work. It's as well that they got what they did. 'Teach 'em more than half-a-dozen rifle flirtations, that will—later—run alone and bite. Poor old Colonel, though.'

All that afternoon the heliograph winked and flickered on the hills, striving to tell the good news to a mountain forty miles away. And in the evening there arrived, dusty, sweating, and sore, a misguided Correspondent, who had gone out to assist at a trumpery village-burning, and who had read off the message from afar, cursing his luck the while.

'Let's have the details somehow—as full as ever you can, please. It's the first time I've ever been left this campaign,' said the Correspondent to the Brigadier, and the Brigadier, nothing loath, told him how an Army of Communication had been crumpled up, destroyed, and all but annihilated by the craft, strategy, wisdom, and foresight of the Brigadier.

But some say, and among these be the Gurkhas who watched on the hillside, that that battle was won by Jakin and Lew, whose little bodies were borne up just in time to fit two gaps at the head of the big ditch-grave for the dead under the heights of Jagai.

THE MAN WHO WAS

The Earth gave up her dead that tide,
    Into our camp he came,
And said his say, and went his way,
    And left our hearts aflame.

Keep tally—on the gun-butt score
    The vengeance we must take,
When God shall bring full reckoning,
    For our dead comrade's sake.
                    Ballad.

LET it be clearly understood that the Russian is a delightful person till he tucks in his shirt. As an Oriental he is charming. It is only when he insists upon being treated as the most easterly of western peoples instead of the most westerly of easterns that he becomes a racial anomaly extremely difficult to handle. The host never knows which side of his nature is going to turn up next.

Dirkovitch was a Russian—a Russian of the Russians—who appeared to get his bread by serving the Czar as an officer in a Cossack regiment, and corresponding for a Russian newspaper with a name that was never twice alike. He was a handsome young Oriental, fond of wandering through unexplored portions of the earth, and he arrived in India from nowhere in particular. At least no living man could ascertain whether it was by way of Balkh, Badakshan, Chitral, Beluchistan, or Nepaul, or anywhere else. The Indian Government, being in an unusually affable mood, gave orders that he was to be civilly treated and shown everything that was to be seen. So he drifted, talking bad English and worse French, from one city to another, till he foregathered with Her Majesty's White Hussars in the city of Peshawur, which stands at the mouth of that narrow swordcut in the hills that men call the Khyber Pass. He was undoubtedly an officer, and he was decorated after the manner of the Russians with little enamelled crosses, and he could talk, and (though this has nothing to do with his merits) he had been given up as a hopeless task, or cask, by the Black Tyrone, who individually and collectively, with hot whisky and honey, mulled brandy, and mixed spirits of every kind, had striven in all hospitality to make him drunk. And when the Black Tyrone, who are exclusively Irish, fail to disturb the peace of head of a foreigner—that foreigner is certain to be a superior man.

The White Hussars were as conscientious in choosing their wine as in charging the enemy. All that they possessed, including some wondrous brandy, was placed at the absolute disposition of Dirkovitch, and he enjoyed himself hugely—even more than among the Black Tyrones.

But he remained distressingly European through it all. The White Hussars were 'My dear true friends,' 'Fellow-soldiers glorious,' and 'Brothers inseparable.' He would unburden himself by the

hour on the glorious future that awaited the combined arms of England and Russia when their hearts
and their territories should run side by side and the
great mission of civilising Asia should begin. That
was unsatisfactory, because Asia is 'not going to be
civilised after the methods of the West. There is
too much Asia and she is too old. You cannot
reform a lady of many lovers, and Asia has been
insatiable in her flirtations aforetime. She will never
attend Sunday school or learn to vote save with
swords for tickets.

Dirkovitch knew this as well as any one else, but
it suited him to talk special-correspondently and to
make himself as genial as he could. Now and then
he volunteered a little, a very little, information about
his own sotnia of Cossacks, left apparently to look
after themselves somewhere at the back of beyond.
He had done rough work in Central Asia, and had
seen rather more help-yourself fighting than most
men of his years. But he was careful never to
betray his superiority, and more than careful to
praise on all occasions the appearance, drill, uniform,
and organisation of Her Majesty's White Hussars.
And indeed they were a regiment to be admired.
When Lady Durgan, widow of the late Sir John
Durgan, arrived in their station, and after a short
time had been proposed to by every single man at
mess, she put the public sentiment very neatly when
she explained that they were all so nice that unless
she could marry them all, including the colonel and
some majors already married, she was not going to
content herself with one hussar. Wherefore she
wedded a little man in a Rifle Regiment, being by

nature contradictious ; and the White Hussars were going to wear crape on their arms, but compromised by attending the wedding in full force, and lining the aisle with unutterable reproach. She had jilted them all—from Basset-Holmer the senior captain to little Mildred the junior subaltern, who could have given her four thousand a year and a title.

The only persons who did not share the general regard for the White Hussars were a few thousand gentlemen of Jewish extraction who lived across the border, and answered to the name of Paythan. They had once met the regiment officially and for something less than twenty minutes, but the interview, which was complicated with many casualties, had filled them with prejudice. They even called the White Hussars children of the devil and sons of persons whom it would be perfectly impossible to meet in decent society. Yet they were not above making their aversion fill their money-belts. The regiment possessed carbines—beautiful Martini-Henry carbines that would lob a bullet into an enemy's camp at one thousand yards, and were even handier than the long rifle. Therefore they were coveted all along the border, and since demand inevitably breeds supply, they were supplied at the risk of life and limb for exactly their weight in coined silver—seven and one half pounds weight of rupees, or sixteen pounds sterling reckoning the rupee at par. They were stolen at night by snaky-haired thieves who crawled on their stomachs under the nose of the sentries ; they disappeared mysteriously from locked arm-racks, and in the hot weather, when all the barrack doors and windows were open, they vanished like puffs of

their own smoke. The border people desired them
for family vendettas and contingencies. But in the
long cold nights of the northern Indian winter they
were stolen most extensively. The traffic of murder
was liveliest among the hills at that season, and
prices ruled high. The regimental guards were first
doubled and then trebled. A trooper does not much
care if he loses a weapon—Government must make
it good—but he deeply resents the loss of his sleep.
The regiment grew very angry, and one rifle-thief
bears the visible marks of their anger upon him to
this hour. That incident stopped the burglaries for
a time, and the guards were reduced accordingly, and
the regiment devoted itself to polo with unexpected
results ; for it beat by two goals to one that very
terrible polo corps the Lushkar Light Horse, though the
latter had four ponies apiece for a short hour's fight,
as well as a native officer who played like a lambent
flame across the ground.

They gave a dinner to celebrate the event. The
Lushkar team came, and Dirkovitch came, in the
fullest full uniform of a Cossack officer, which is as
full as a dressing-gown, and was introduced to the
Lushkars, and opened his eyes as he regarded. They
were lighter men than the Hussars, and they carried
themselves with the swing that is the peculiar right
of the Punjab Frontier Force and all Irregular Horse.
Like everything else in the Service it has to be learnt,
but, unlike many things, it is never forgotten, and
remains on the body till death.

The great beam-roofed mess-room of the White
Hussars was a sight to be remembered. All the
mess plate was out on the long table—the same

table that had served up the bodies of five officers
after a forgotten fight long and long ago—the dingy,
battered standards faced the door of entrance, clumps
of winter-roses lay between the silver candlesticks,
and the portraits of eminent officers deceased looked
down on their successors from between the heads of
sambhur, nilghai, markhor, and, pride of all the mess,
two grinning snow-leopards that had cost Basset-
Holmer four months' leave that he might have spent
in England, instead of on the road to Thibet and the
daily risk of his life by ledge, snow-slide, and grassy
slope.

The servants in spotless white muslin and the
crest of their regiments on the brow of their turbans
waited behind their masters, who were clad in the
scarlet and gold of the White Hussars, and the
cream and silver of the Lushkar Light Horse.
Dirkovitch's dull green uniform was the only dark
spot at the board, but his big onyx eyes made up for
it. He was fraternising effusively with the Captain
of the Lushkar team, who was wondering how many
of Dirkovitch's Cossacks his own dark wiry down-
country-men could account for in a fair charge. But
one does not speak of these things openly.

The talk rose higher and higher, and the Regimental Band played between the courses, as is the
immemorial custom, till all tongues ceased for a
moment with the removal of the dinner-slips and
the first toast of obligation, when an officer rising
said, 'Mr. Vice, the Queen,' and little Mildred from
the bottom of the table answered, 'The Queen, God
bless her,' and the big spurs clanked as the big men
heaved themselves up and drank the Queen upon

whose pay they were falsely supposed to settle their
mess-bills.   That Sacrament of the Mess never grows
old, and never ceases to bring a lump into the throat
of the listener wherever he be by sea or by land.
Dirkovitch rose with his 'brothers glorious,' but he
could not understand.   No one but an officer can
tell what the toast means ; and the bulk have more
sentiment than comprehension.   Immediately after
the little silence that follows on the ceremony there
entered the native officer who had played for the
Lushkar team.   He could not, of course, eat with
the mess, but he came in at desert, all six feet of
him, with the blue and silver turban atop, and the
big black boots below.   The mess rose joyously as he
thrust forward the hilt of his sabre in token of fealty
for the Colonel of the White Hussars to touch, and
dropped into a vacant chair amid shouts of : '*Rung
ho*, Hira Singh !' (which being translated means 'Go
in and win ').   'Did I whack you over the knee, old
man ? '   'Ressaidar Sahib, what the devil made you
play that kicking pig of a pony in the last ten
minutes ? '   '*Shabash*, Ressaidar Sahib !'   Then the
voice of the Colonel, 'The health of Ressaidar Hira
Singh !'

After the shouting had died away Hira Singh
rose to reply, for he was the cadet of a royal house,
the son of a king's son, and knew what was due on
these occasions.   Thus he spoke in the vernacular :—
'Colonel Sahib and officers of this regiment.   Much
honour have you done me.   This will I remember.
We came down from afar to play you.   But we were
beaten ' (' No fault of yours, Ressaidar Sahib.   Played
on our own ground y' know.   Your ponies were

'*Rung ho*, Hira Singh!'—P. 72.

cramped from the railway. Don't apologise!')
'Therefore perhaps we will come again if it be so
ordained.' ('Hear! Hear! Hear, indeed! Bravo!
Hsh!') 'Then we will play you afresh' ('Happy to
meet you.') 'till there are left no feet upon our ponies.
Thus far for sport.' He dropped one hand on his
sword-hilt and his eye wandered to Dirkovitch lolling
back in his chair. 'But if by the will of God there
arises any other game which is not the polo game,
then be assured, Colonel Sahib and officers, that we
will play it out side by side, though *they*,' again
his eye sought Dirkovitch, 'though *they* I say
have fifty ponies to our one horse.' And with a
deep-mouthed *Rung ho!* that sounded like a
musket-butt on flagstones he sat down amid leaping glasses.

Dirkovitch, who had devoted himself steadily to
the brandy—the terrible brandy aforementioned—
did not understand, nor did the expurgated trans-
lations offered to him at all convey the point. De-
cidedly Hira Singh's was the speech of the evening,
and the clamour might have continued to the dawn
had it not been broken by the noise of a shot
without that sent every man feeling at his defence-
less left side. Then there was a scuffle and a yell
of pain.

'Carbine-stealing again!' said the Adjutant, calmly
sinking back in his chair. 'This comes of reducing
the guards. I hope the sentries have killed him.'

The feet of armed men pounded on the veranda
flags, and it was as though something was being
dragged.

'Why don't they put him in the cells till the

morning?' said the Colonel testily. 'See if they've damaged him, Sergeant.'

The Mess-Sergeant fled out into the darkness and returned with two troopers and a corporal, all very much perplexed.

'Caught a man stealin' carbines, Sir,' said the Corporal. 'Leastways 'e was crawlin' towards the barricks, Sir, past the main road sentries, an' the sentry 'e sez, Sir——'

The limp heap of rags upheld by the three men groaned. Never was seen so destitute and demoralised an Afghan. He was turbanless, shoeless, caked with dirt, and all but dead with rough handling. Hira Singh started slightly at the sound of the man's pain. Dirkovitch took another glass of brandy.

'*What* does the sentry say?' said the Colonel.

'Sez 'e speaks English, Sir,' said the Corporal.

'So you brought him into mess instead of handing him over to the Sergeant! If he spoke all the Tongues of the Pentecost you've no business——'

Again the bundle groaned and muttered. Little Mildred had risen from his place to inspect. He jumped back as though he had been shot.

● 'Perhaps it would be better, Sir, to send the men away,' said he to the Colonel, for he was a much privileged subaltern. He put his arms round the rag-bound horror as he spoke, and dropped him into a chair. It may not have been explained that the littleness of Mildred lay in his being six feet four and big in proportion. The Corporal seeing that an officer was disposed to look after the capture, and that the Colonel's eye was beginning to blaze, promptly removed himself and his men. The mess was left alone with the carbine-thief, who laid his head on the table and wept bitterly, hopelessly, and inconsolably, as little children weep.

Hira Singh leapt to his feet. 'Colonel Sahib,' said he, 'that man is no Afghan, for they weep *Ai!* *Ai!* Nor is he of Hindustan, for they weep *Oh!* *Ho!* He weeps after the fashion of the white men, who say *Ow! Ow!*'

'Now where the dickens did you get that knowledge, Hira Singh?' said the Captain of the Lushkar team.

'Hear him!' said Hira Singh simply, pointing at the crumpled figure that wept as though it would never cease.

'He said, "My God!"' said little Mildred. 'I heard him say it.'

The Colonel and the mess-room looked at the man in silence. It is a horrible thing to hear a man cry. A woman can sob from the top of her palate, or her lips, or anywhere else, but a man must cry from his diaphragm, and it rends him to pieces.

'Poor devil!' said the Colonel, coughing tremendously. 'We ought to send him to hospital. He's been man-handled.'

Now the Adjutant loved his carbines. They were to him as his grandchildren, the men standing in the first place. He grunted rebelliously: 'I can understand an Afghan stealing, because he's built that way. But I can't understand his crying. That makes it worse.'

The brandy must have affected Dirkovitch, for he lay back in his chair and stared at the ceiling.

There was nothing special in the ceiling beyond a shadow as of a huge black coffin. Owing to some peculiarity in the construction of the mess-room this shadow was always thrown when the candles were lighted. It never disturbed the digestion of the White Hussars. They were in fact rather proud of it.

'Is he going to cry all night?' said the Colonel, 'or are we supposed to sit up with little Mildred's guest until he feels better?'

The man in the chair threw up his head and stared at the mess. 'Oh, my God!' he said, and every soul in the mess rose to his feet. Then the Lushkar Captain did a deed for which he ought to have been given the Victoria Cross—distinguished gallantry in a fight against overwhelming curiosity. He picked up his team with his eyes as the hostess picks up the ladies at the opportune moment, and pausing only by the Colonel's chair to say, 'This isn't *our* affair, you know, Sir,' led them into the veranda and the gardens. Hira Singh was the last to go, and he looked at Dirkovitch. But Dirkovitch had departed into a brandy-paradise of his own. His lips moved without sound and he was studying the coffin on the ceiling.

'White—white all over,' said Basset-Holmer, the Adjutant. 'What a pernicious renegade he must be! I wonder where he came from?'

The Colonel shook the man gently by the arm, and 'Who are you?' said he.

There was no answer. The man stared round the mess-room and smiled in the Colonel's face. Little Mildred, who was always more of a woman

He found the spring. —P. 77.

than a man till 'Boot and saddle' was sounded, repeated the question in a voice that would have drawn confidences from a geyser. The man only smiled. Dirkovitch at the far end of the table slid gently from his chair to the floor. No son of Adam in this present imperfect world can mix the Hussars' champagne with the Hussars' brandy by five and eight glasses of each without remembering the pit whence he was digged and descending thither. The Band began to play the tune with which the White Hussars from the date of their formation have concluded all their functions. They would sooner be disbanded than abandon that tune; it is a part of their system. The man straightened himself in his chair and drummed on the table with his fingers.

'I don't see why we should entertain lunatics,' said the Colonel. 'Call a guard and send him off to the cells. We'll look into the business in the morning. Give him a glass of wine first though.'

Little Mildred filled a sherry - glass with the brandy and thrust it over to the man. He drank, and the tune rose louder, and he straightened himself yet more. Then he put out his long-taloned hands to a piece of plate opposite and fingered it lovingly. There was a mystery connected with that piece of plate, in the shape of a spring which converted what was a seven-branched candlestick, three springs on each side and one in the middle, into a sort of wheel-spoke candelabrum. He found the spring, pressed it, and laughed weakly. He rose from his chair and inspected a picture on the wall, then moved on to another picture, the mess watching him without a word. When he came to the mantelpiece he shook his head and seemed distressed. A piece of plate representing a mounted hussar in full uniform caught his eye. He pointed to it, and then to the mantelpiece with inquiry in his eyes.

'What is it—Oh what is it?' said little Mildred. Then as a mother might speak to a child, 'That is a horse. Yes, a horse.'

Very slowly came the answer in a thick, passionless guttural—'Yes, I—have seen. But—where is *the* horse?'

You could have heard the hearts of the mess beating as the men drew back to give the stranger full room in his wanderings. There was no question of calling the guard.

Again he spoke—very slowly, 'Where is *our* horse?'

There is but one horse in the White Hussars, and his portrait hangs outside the door of the mess-room. He is the piebald drum-horse, the king of the Regimental Band, that served the Regiment for seven-and-thirty years, and in the end was shot for old age. Half the mess tore the thing down from its place and thrust it into the man's hands. He placed it above the mantelpiece, it clattered on the ledge as his poor hands dropped it, and he staggered towards the bottom of the table, falling into Mildred's chair. Then all the men spoke to one another something after this fashion, 'The drum-horse hasn't hung over the mantelpiece since '67.' 'How does he know?' 'Mildred, go and speak to him again.' 'Colonel, what are you going to do?' 'Oh, dry up, and give the poor devil a chance to pull himself together.' 'It isn't possible anyhow. The man's a lunatic.'

Little Mildred stood at the Colonel's side talking in his ear. 'Will you be good enough to take your seats, please, gentlemen!' he said, and the mess dropped into the chairs. Only Dirkovitch's seat, next to little Mildred's, was blank, and little Mildred himself had found Hira Singh's place. The wide-eyed Mess-Sergeant filled the glasses in dead silence. Once more the Colonel rose, but his hand shook, and the port spilled on the table as he looked straight at the man in little Mildred's chair and said hoarsely, 'Mr. Vice, the Queen.' There was a little pause, but the man sprung to his feet and answered without hesitation, 'The Queen, God bless her!' and as he emptied the thin glass he snapped the shank between his fingers.

Long and long ago, when the Empress of India was a young woman and there were no unclean ideals in the land, it was the custom of a few messes to drink the Queen's toast in broken glass, to the vast delight of the mess-contractors. The custom is now dead, because there is nothing to break anything for, except now and again the word of a Government, and that has been broken already.

'That settles it,' said the Colonel, with a gasp. 'He's not a sergeant. What in the world is he?'

The entire mess echoed the word, and the volley of questions would have scared any man. It was no wonder that the ragged, filthy invader could only smile and shake his head.

From under the table, calm and smiling, rose Dirkovitch, who had been roused from healthful slumber by feet upon his body. By the side of the man he rose, and the man shrieked and grovelled.

It was a horrible sight coming so swiftly upon the pride and glory of the toast that had brought the strayed wits together.

Dirkovitch made no offer to raise him, but little Mildred heaved him up in an instant. It is not good that a gentleman who can answer to the Queen's toast should lie at the feet of a subaltern of Cossacks.

The hasty action tore the wretch's upper clothing nearly to the waist, and his body was seamed with dry black scars. There is only one weapon in the world that cuts in parallel lines, and it is neither the cane nor the cat. Dirkovitch saw the marks, and the pupils of his eyes dilated. Also his face changed. He said something that sounded like *Shto ve takete*, and the man fawning answered, *Chetyre*.

'What's that?' said everybody together.

'His number. That is number four, you know,' Dirkovitch spoke very thickly.

'What has a Queen's officer to do with a qualified number?' said the Colonel, and an unpleasant growl ran round the table.

'How can I tell?' said the affable Oriental with a sweet smile. 'He is a—how you have it?— escape—run-a-way, from over there.' He nodded towards the darkness of the night.

'Speak to him if he'll answer you, and speak to him gently,' said little Mildred, settling the man in a chair. It seemed most improper to all present that Dirkovitch should sip brandy as he talked in purring, spitting Russian to the creature who answered so feebly and with such evident dread. But

It is not good that a gentleman who can answer to the Queen's toast should lie at the feet of a subaltern of Cossacks. —P. 80.

since Dirkovitch appeared to understand no one said a word. All breathed heavily, leaning forward, in the long gaps of the conversation. The next time that they have no engagements on hand the White Hussars intend to go to St. Petersburg in a body to learn Russian.

'He does not know how many years ago,' said Dirkovitch facing the mess, 'but he says it was very long ago in a war. I think that there was an accident. He says he was of this glorious and distinguished Regiment in the war.'

'The rolls! The rolls! Holmer, get the rolls!' said little Mildred, and the Adjutant dashed off bareheaded to the orderly-room, where the muster-rolls of the Regiment were kept. He returned just in time to hear Dirkovitch conclude, 'Therefore, my dear friends, I am most sorry to say there was an accident which would have been reparable if he had apologised to that our colonel, which he had insulted.'

Then followed another growl which the Colonel tried to beat down. The mess was in no mood just then to weigh insults to Russian colonels.

'He does not remember, but I think that there was an accident, and so he was not exchanged among the prisoners, but he was sent to another place—how do you say?—the country. *So*, he says, he came here. He does not know how he came. Eh? He was at Chepany'—the man caught the word, nodded, and shivered—'at Zhigansk and Irkutsk. I cannot understand how he escaped. He says, too, that he was in the forests for many years, but how many years he has forgotten—that with

G

many things. It was an accident; done because he did not apologise to that our colonel. Ah !'

Instead of echoing Dirkovitch's sigh of regret, it is sad to record that the White Hussars livelily exhibited un-Christian delight and other emotions, hardly restrained by their sense of hospitality. Holmer flung the frayed and yellow regimental rolls on the table, and the men flung themselves at these.

'Steady! Fifty-six—fifty-five—fifty-four,' said Holmer. 'Here we are. "Lieutenant Austin Limmason. *Missing.*" That was before Sebastopol. What an infernal shame! Insulted one of their colonels, and was quietly shipped off. Thirty years of his life wiped out.'

'But he never apologised. Said he'd see him damned first,' chorused the mess.

'Poor chap! I suppose he never had the chance afterwards. How did he come here?' said the Colonel.

The dingy heap in the chair could give no answer.

'Do you know who you are?'

It laughed weakly.

'Do you know that you are Limmason—Lieutenant Limmason of the White Hussars?'

Swiftly as a shot came the answer, in a slightly surprised tone, 'Yes, I'm Limmason, of course.' The light died out in his eyes, and the man collapsed, watching every motion of Dirkovitch with terror. A flight from Siberia may fix a few elementary facts in the mind, but it does not seem to lead to continuity of thought. The man could not explain how, like a homing pigeon, he had found his way to his own old mess again. Of what he had

suffered or seen he knew nothing. He cringed
before Dirkovitch as instinctively as he had pressed
the spring of the candlestick, sought the picture of
the drum-horse, and answered to the toast of the
Queen. The rest was a blank that the dreaded
Russian tongue could only in part remove. His
head bowed on his breast, and he giggled and
cowered alternately.

The devil that lived in the brandy prompted
Dirkovitch at this extremely inopportune moment to
make a speech. He rose, swaying slightly, gripped
the table-edge, while his eyes glowed like opals, and
began :

' Fellow-soldiers glorious—true friends and hos-
pitables. It was an accident, and deplorable—most
deplorable.' Here he smiled sweetly all round the
mess. ' But you will think of this little, little thing.
So little, is it not ? The Czar ! Posh ! I slap my
fingers—I snap my fingers at him. Do I believe in
him ? No ! But in us Slav who has done nothing,
him I believe. Seventy — how much — millions
peoples that have done nothing—not one thing.
Posh ! Napoleon was an episode.' He banged a
hand on the table. ' Hear you, old peoples, we have
done nothing in the world—out here. All our work
is to do ; and it shall be done, old peoples. Get
a-way !' He waved his hand imperiously, and
pointed to the man. ' You see him. He is not
good to see. He was just one little—oh, so little—
accident, that no one remembered. Now he is
That ! So will you be, brother soldiers so brave—
so will you be.' But you will never come back.
You will all go where he is gone, or '—he pointed to

the great coffin-shadow on the ceiling, and muttering, 'Seventy millions—get a-way, you old peoples,' fell asleep.

'Sweet, and to the point,' said little Mildred. 'What's the use of getting wroth? Let's make this poor devil comfortable.'

But that was a matter suddenly and swiftly taken from the loving hands of the White Hussars. The lieutenant had returned only to go away again three days later, when the wail of the Dead March, and the tramp of the squadrons, told the wondering Station, who saw no gap in the mess-table, that an officer of the Regiment had resigned his new-found commission.

And Dirkovitch, bland, supple, and always genial, went away too by a night train. Little Mildred and another man saw him off, for he was the guest of the mess, and even had he smitten the Colonel with the open hand, the law of that mess allowed no relaxation of hospitality.

'Good-bye, Dirkovitch, and a pleasant journey,' said little Mildred.

'*Au revoir*,' said the Russian.

'Indeed! But we thought you were going home?'

'Yes, but I will come again. My dear friends, is that road shut?' He pointed to where the North Star burned over the Khyber Pass.

'By Jove! I forgot. Of course. Happy to meet you, old man, any time you like. Got everything you want? Cheroots, ice, bedding? That's all right. Well, *au revoir*, Dirkovitch.'

'Um,' said the other man, as the tail-lights of

the train grew small. 'Of — all — the — unmitigated——!'

Little Mildred answered nothing, but watched the
North Star and hummed a selection from a recent
Simla burlesque that had much delighted the White
Hussars. It ran—

> I'm sorry for Mister Bluebeard,
> I'm sorry to cause him pain ;
> But a terrible spree there's sure to be
> When he comes back again.

THE COURTING OF DINAH SHADD

What did the colonel's lady think ?
  Nobody never knew.
Somebody asked the sergeant's wife
  An' she told 'em true.
When you git to a man in the case
  They're like a row o' pins,
For the colonel's lady an' Judy O'Grady
  Are sisters under their skins.
                Barrack Room Ballad.

ALL day I had followed at the heels of a pursuing army engaged on one of the finest battles that ever camp of exercise beheld.   Thirty thousand troops had by the wisdom of the Government of India been turned loose over a few thousand square miles of country to practise in peace what they would never attempt in war.   Consequently cavalry charged unshaken infantry at the trot.   Infantry captured artillery by frontal attacks delivered in line of quarter columns, and mounted infantry skirmished up to the wheels of an armoured train which carried nothing more deadly than a twenty-five pounder Armstrong, two Nordenfeldts, and a few score volunteers all cased in three-eighths-inch boiler-plate.   Yet it was a very lifelike camp.   Operations did not cease at sundown ;

nobody knew the country and nobody spared man
or horse.   There was unending cavalry scouting and
almost unending forced work over broken ground.
The Army of the South had finally pierced the
centre of the Army of the North, and was pouring
through the gap hot-foot to capture a city of
strategic importance.   Its front extended fanwise,
the sticks being represented by regiments strung out
along the line of route backwards to the divisional
transport columns and all the lumber that trails
behind an army on the move.   On its right the
broken left of the Army of the North was flying in
mass, chased by the Southern horse and hammered
by the Southern guns till these had been pushed far
beyond the limits of their last support.   Then the
flying sat down to rest, while the elated commandant
of the pursuing force telegraphed that he held all in
check and observation.

Unluckily he did not observe that three miles to
his right flank a flying column of Northern horse
with a detachment of Gurkhas and British troops
had been pushed round, as fast as the failing light
allowed, to cut across the entire rear of the Southern
Army, to break, as it were, all the ribs of the fan
where they converged by striking at the transport,
reserve ammunition, and artillery supplies.   Their
instructions were to go in, avoiding the few scouts
who might not have been drawn off by the pursuit,
and create sufficient excitement to impress the
Southern Army with the wisdom of guarding their
own flank and rear before they captured cities.   It
was a pretty manœuvre, neatly carried out.

Speaking for the second division of the Southern

Army, our first intimation of the attack was at twilight, when the artillery were labouring in deep sand, most of the escort were trying to help them out, and the main body of the infantry had gone on. A Noah's Ark of elephants, camels, and the mixed menagerie of an Indian transport-train bubbled and squealed behind the guns, when there appeared from nowhere in particular British infantry to the extent of three companies, who sprang to the heads of the gun-horses and brought all to a standstill amid oaths and cheers.

'How's that, umpire?' said the Major commanding the attack, and with one voice the drivers and limber gunners answered 'Hout!' while the Colonel of Artillery sputtered.

'All your scouts are charging our main body,' said the Major. 'Your flanks are unprotected for two miles. I think we've broken the back of this division. And listen,—there go the Gurkhas!'

A weak fire broke from the rear-guard more than a mile away, and was answered by cheerful howlings. The Gurkhas, who should have swung clear of the second division, had stepped on its tail in the dark, but drawing off hastened to reach the next line of attack, which lay almost parallel to us five or six miles away.

Our column swayed and surged irresolutely,— three batteries, the divisional ammunition reserve, the baggage, and a section of the hospital and bearer corps. The commandant ruefully promised to report himself 'cut up' to the nearest umpire, and commending his cavalry and all other cavalry to the special care of Eblis, toiled on to resume touch with the rest of the division.

'We'll bivouac here to-night,' said the Major; 'I have a notion that the Gurkhas will get caught. They may want us to re-form on. Stand easy till the transport gets away.'

A hand caught my beast's bridle and led him out of the choking dust; a larger hand deftly canted me out of the saddle; and two of the hugest hands in the world received me sliding. Pleasant is the lot of the special correspondent who falls into such hands as those of Privates Mulvaney, Ortheris, and Learoyd.

'An' that's all right,' said the Irishman calmly. 'We thought we'd find you somewheres here by. Is there anything av yours in the transport? Orth'ris 'll fetch ut out.'

Ortheris did 'fetch ut out,' from under the trunk of an elephant, in the shape of a servant and an animal both laden with medical comforts. The little man's eyes sparkled.

'If the brutil an' licentious soldiery av these parts gets sight av the thruck,' said Mulvaney, making practised investigation, 'they'll loot ev'rything. They're bein' fed on iron-filin's an' dog-biscuit these days, but glory's no compensation for a belly-ache. Praise be, we're here to protect you, Sorr. Beer, sausage, bread (soft an' that's a cur'osity), soup in a tin, whisky by the smell av ut, an' fowls! Mother av Moses, but ye take the field like a confectioner! T'is scand'lus.'

''Ere's a orficer,' said Ortheris significantly. 'When the sergent's done lushin' the privit may clean the pot.'

I bundled several things into Mulvaney's haversack

before the Major's hand fell on my shoulder and he said tenderly, ' Requisitioned for the Queen's service. Wolseley was quite wrong about special correspondents : they are the soldier's best friends. Come and take pot-luck with us to-night.'

And so it happened amid laughter and shoutings that my well-considered commissariat melted away to reappear later at the mess-table, which was a waterproof sheet spread on the ground. The flying column had taken three days' rations with it, and there be few things nastier than Government rations —especially when Government is experimenting with German toys. Erbswurst, tinned beef of surpassing tinniness, compressed vegetables, and meat-biscuits may be nourishing, but what Thomas Atkins needs is bulk in his inside. The Major, assisted by his brother officers, purchased goats for the camp and so made the experiment of no effect. Long before the fatigue-party sent to collect brushwood had returned, the men were settled down by their valises, kettles and pots had appeared from the surrounding country and were dangling over fires as the kid and the compressed vegetable bubbled together ; there rose a cheerful clinking of mess-tins ; outrageous demands for ' a little more stuffin' with that there liver-wing ' ; and gust on gust of chaff as pointed as a bayonet and as delicate as a gun-butt.

' The boys are in a good temper,' said the Major. ' They'll be singing presently. Well, a night like this is enough to keep them happy.'

Over our heads burned the wonderful Indian stars, which are not all pricked in on one plane, but, preserving an orderly perspective, draw the eye through the velvet darkness of the void up to the barred doors of heaven itself. The earth was a gray shadow more unreal than the sky. We could hear her breathing lightly in the pauses between the howling of the jackals, the movement of the wind in the tamarisks, and the fitful mutter of musketry-fire leagues away to the left. A native woman from some unseen hut began to sing, the mail-train thundered past on its way to Delhi, and a roosting crow cawed drowsily. Then there was a belt-loosening silence about the fires, and the even breathing of the crowded earth took up the story.

The men, full fed, turned to tobacco and song,—their officers with them. The subaltern is happy who can win the approval of the musical critics in his regiment, and is honoured among the more intricate step-dancers. By him, as by him who plays cricket cleverly, Thomas Atkins will stand in time of need, when he will let a better officer go on alone. The ruined tombs of forgotten Mussulman saints heard the ballad of *Agra Town, The Buffalo Battery, Marching to Kabul, The long, long Indian Day, The Place where the Punkah-coolie died*, and that crashing chorus which announces,

> Youth's daring spirit, manhood's fire,
> Firm hand and eagle eye,
> Must he acquire, who would aspire
> To see the gray boar die.

To-day, of all those jovial thieves who appropriated my commissariat and lay and laughed round that waterproof sheet, not one remains. They went to camps that were not of exercise and battles

without empires. Burma, the Soudan, and the
frontier, — fever and fight, — took them in their
time.

I drifted across to the men's fires in search of
Mulvaney, whom I found strategically greasing his feet
by the blaze. There is nothing particularly lovely in
the sight of a private thus engaged after a long day's
march, but when you reflect on the exact proportion
of the 'might, majesty, dominion, and power' of the
British Empire which stands on those feet you take
an interest in the proceedings.

'There's a blister, bad luck to ut, on the heel,'
said Mulvaney. 'I can't touch ut. Prick ut out,
little man.'

Ortheris took out his house - wife, eased the
trouble with a needle, stabbed Mulvaney in the calf
with the same weapon, and was swiftly kicked into
the fire.

'I've bruk the best av my toes over you, ye
grinnin' child av disruption,' said Mulvaney, sitting
cross-legged and nursing his feet; then seeing me,
'Oh, ut's you, Sorr! Be welkim, an' take that
maraudin' scutt's place. Jock, hold him down on
the cindhers for a bit.'

But Ortheris escaped and went elsewhere, as I
took possession of the hollow he had scraped for
himself and lined with his greatcoat. Learoyd on
the other side of the fire grinned affably and in a
minute fell fast asleep.

'There's the height av politeness for you,' said
Mulvaney, lighting his pipe with a flaming branch.
'But Jock's eaten half a box av your sardines at
wan gulp, an' I think the tin too. What's the best

wid you, Sorr, an' how did you happen to be on the
losin' side this day whin we captured you?'

'The Army of the South is winning all along the
line,' I said.

'Then that line's the hangman's rope, savin' your
presince. You'll learn to-morrow how we rethreated
to dhraw thim on before we made thim trouble, an'
that's what a woman does. By the same tokin,
we'll be attacked before the dawnin' an' ut would be
betther not to slip your boots. How do I know
that? By the light av pure reason. Here are
three companies av us ever so far inside av the
enemy's flank an' a crowd av roarin', tarin', squealin'
cavalry gone on just to turn out the whole hornet's
nest av them. Av course the enemy will pursue, by
brigades like as not, an' thin we'll have to run for ut.
Mark my words. I am av the opinion av Polonius
whin he said, "Don't fight wid ivry scutt for the
pure joy av fightin', but if you do, knock the nose
av him first and frequint." We ought to ha' gone
on an' helped the Gurkhas.'

'But what do you know about Polonius?' I
demanded. This was a new side of Mulvaney's
character.

'All that Shakespeare iver wrote an' a dale more
that the gallery shouted,' said the man of war, carefully lacing his boots. 'Did I not tell you av
Silver's Theatre in Dublin, whin I was younger than I
am now an' a patron av the drama? Ould Silver
wud never pay actor-man or woman their just dues,
an' by consequince his comp'nies was collapsible at
the last minut. Thin the bhoys wud clamour to
take a part, an' oft as not ould Silver made them

pay for the fun. Faith, I've seen Hamlut played wid a new black eye an' the queen as full as a cornucopia. I remimber wanst Hogin that 'listed in the Black Tyrone an' was shot in South Africa, he sejuced ould Silver into givin' him Hamlut's part instid av me that had a fine fancy for rhetoric in those days. Av course I wint into the gallery an' began to fill the pit wid other peoples' hats, an' I passed the time av day to Hogin walkin' through Denmark like a hamstrung mule wid a pall on his back. " Hamlut," sez I, " there's a hole in your heel. Pull up your shtockin's, Hamlut," sez I. " Hamlut, Hamlut, for the love av decincy dhrop that skull an' pull up your shtockin's." The whole house begun to tell him that. He stopped his soliloquishms mid-betwcen. " My shtockin's may be comin' down or they may not," sez he, screwin' his eye into the gallery, for well he knew who I was. " But afther this performince is over me an' the Ghost 'll trample the tripes out av you, Terence, wid your ass's bray ! " An' that's how I come to know about Hamlut. Eyah ! Those days, those days ! Did you iver have onendin' devilmint an' nothin' to pay for it in your life, Sorr ? '

'Never, without having to pay,' I said.

'That's thrue ! 'Tis mane whin you considher on ut ; but ut's the same wid horse or fut. A head-ache if you dhrink, an' a belly-ache if you eat too much, an' a heart-ache to kape all down. Faith, the beast only gets the colic, an' he's the lucky man.'

He dropped his head and stared into the fire, fingering his moustache the while. From the far side of the bivouac the voice of Corbet-Nolan, senior subaltern of B company, uplifted itself in an ancient and much-appreciated song of sentiment, the men moaning melodiously behind him.

The north wind blew coldly, she drooped from that hour,
My own little Kathleen, my sweet little Kathleen,
Kathleen, my Kathleen, Kathleen O'Moore!

With forty-five O's in the last word : even at that distance you might have cut the soft South Irish accent with a shovel.

'For all we take we must pay, but the price is cruel high,' murmured Mulvaney when the chorus had ceased.

'What's the trouble?' I said gently, for I knew that he was a man of an inextinguishable sorrow.

'Hear now,' said he. 'Ye know what I am now. *I* know what I mint to be at the beginnin' av my service. I've tould you time an' again, an' what I have not Dinah Shadd has. An' what am I? Oh, Mary Mother av Hiven, an ould dhrunken, untrustable baste av a privit that has seen the Rig'ment change out from colonel to drummer-boy, not wanst or twice, but scores av times! Ay, scores! An' me not so near gettin' promotion as in the first! An' me livin' on an' kapin' clear av clink, not by my own good conduck, but the kindness av some orf'cer-bhoy young enough to be son to me! Do I not know ut? Can I not tell whin I'm passed over at p'rade, tho' I'm rockin' full av liquor an' ready to fall all in wan piece, such as even a suckin' child might see, bekaze, "Oh, 'tis only ould Mulvaney!" An' whin I'm let off in ord'ly-room through some

thrick of the tongue an' a ready answer an' the ould
man's mercy, is ut smilin' I feel whin I fall away an'
go back to Dinah Shadd, thryin' to carry ut all off
as a joke? Not I! 'Tis hell to me, dumb hell
through ut all ; an' next time whin the fit comes I
will be as bad again. Good cause the Rig'ment has to
know me for the best soldier in ut. Better cause have
I to know mesilf for the worst man. I'm only fit to
tache the new drafts what I'll niver learn myself;
an' I am sure, as tho' I heard ut, that the minut
wan av these pink-eyed recruities gets away from
my " Mind ye now," an' " Listen to this, Jim, bhoy,"
—sure I am that the sargint houlds me up to him
for a warnin'. So I tache, as they say at musketry-
instruction, by direct and ricochet fire. Lord be
good to me, for I have stud some throuble !'

'Lie down and go to sleep,' said I, not being able
to comfort or advise. ' You're the best man in the
Regiment, and, next to Ortheris, the biggest fool.
Lie down and wait till we're attacked. What force
will they turn out ? Guns, think you ?'

'Try that wid your lorrds an' ladies, twistin' an'
turnin' the talk, tho' you mint ut well. Ye cud
say nothin' to help me, an' yet ye niver knew what
cause I had to be what I am.'

'Begin at the beginning and go on to the end,' I
said royally. 'But rake up the fire a bit first.'

I passed Ortheris's bayonet for a poker.

'That shows how little we know what we do,'
said Mulvaney, putting it aside. ' Fire takes all the
heart out av the steel, an' the next time, maybe,
that our little man is fighting for his life his
bradawl 'll break, an' so you'll ha' killed him, manin'

no more than to kape yourself warm. 'Tis a recruity's thrick that. Pass the clanin'-rod, Sorr.'

I snuggled down abashed ; and after an interval the voice of Mulvaney began.

'Did I iver tell you how Dinah Shadd came to be wife av mine?'

I dissembled a burning anxiety that I had felt for some months—ever since Dinah Shadd, the strong, the patient, and the infinitely tender, had of her own good love and free will washed a shirt for me, moving in a barren land where washing was not.

'I can't remember,' I said casually. 'Was it before or after you made love to Annie Bragin, and got no satisfaction?'

The story of Annie Bragin is written in another place. It is one of the many less respectable epi-sodes in Mulvaney's chequered career.

'Before—before—long before, was that business av Annie Bragin an' the corp'ril's ghost. Niver woman was the worse for me whin I had married Dinah. There's a time for all things, an' I know how to kape all things in place—barrin' the dhrink, that kapes me in my place wid no hope av comin' to be aught else.'

'Begin at the beginning,' I insisted. 'Mrs. Mulvaney told me that you married her when you were quartered in Krab Bokhar barracks.'

'An' the same is a cess-pit,' said Mulvaney piously. 'She spoke thrue, did Dinah. 'Twas this way. Talkin' av that, have ye iver fallen in love, Sorr?'

I preserved the silence of the damned. Mulvaney continued—

'Thin I will assume that ye have not. _I_ did. In the days av my youth, as I have more than wanst tould you, I was a man that filled the eye an' delighted the sowl av women. Niver man was hated as I have bin. Niver man was loved as I—no, not within half a day's march av ut! For the first five years av my service, whin I was what I wud give my sowl to be now, I tuk whatever was within my reach an' digested ut—an' that's more than most men can say. Dhrink I tuk, an' ut did me no harm. By the Hollow av Hiven, I cud play wid four women at wanst, an' kape them from findin' out anythin' about the other three, an' smile like a full-blown marigold through ut all. Dick Coulhan, av the battery we'll have down on us to-night, could drive his team no better than I mine, an' I hild the worser cattle! An' so I lived, an' so I was happy till afther that business wid Annie Bragin—she that turned me off as cool as a meat-safe, an' taught me where I stud in the mind av an honest woman. 'Twas no sweet dose to swallow.

'Afther that I sickened awhile an' tuk thought to my rig'mintal work; conceiting mesilf I wud study an' be a sargint, an' a major-gineral twinty minutes afther that. But on top av my ambitiousness there was an empty place in my sowl, an' me own opinion av mesilf cud not fill ut. Sez I to mesilf, "Terence, you're a great man an' the best set-up in the rig'mint. Go on an' get promotion." Sez mesilf to me, "What for?" Sez I to mesilf, "For the glory av ut!" Sez mesilf to me, "Will that fill these two strong arrums av yours, Terence?" "Go to the devil," sez I to mesilf. "Go to the married

lines," sez mesilf to me. "'Tis the same thing," sez
I to mesilf. "Av you're the same man, ut is," said
mesilf to me ; an' wid that I considhered on ut a
long while. Did you iver feel that way, Sorr ?'

I snored gently, knowing that if Mulvaney were
uninterrupted he would go on. The clamour from
the bivouac fires beat up to the stars, as the rival
singers of the companies were pitted against each
other.

'So I felt that way an' a bad time ut was.
Wanst, bein' a fool, I wint into the married lines
more for the sake av spakin' to our ould Colour-
Sargint Shadd than for any thruck wid women-folk.
I was a corp'ril then—rejuced aftherwards, but a
corp'ril then. I've got a photograft av mesilf to
prove ut. "You'll take a cup av tay wid us?" sez
Shadd. "I will that," I sez, "tho' tay is not my
divarsion."

'"'Twud be better for you if ut were," sez ould
Mother Shadd, an' she had ought to know, for Shadd,
in the ind av his service, dhrank bung-full each
night.

'Wid that I tuk off my gloves—there was pipe-
clay in thim, so that they stud alone—an' pulled up
my chair, lookin' round at the china ornaments an'
bits av things in the Shadds' quarters. They were
things that belonged to a man, an' no camp-kit, here
to-day and dishipated next. "You're comfortable in
this place, Sargint," sez I. "'Tis the wife that did ut,
boy," sez he, pointin' the stem av his pipe to ould
Mother Shadd, an' she smacked the top av his bald
head apon the compliment. "That manes you want
money," sez she.

'An' thin—an' thin whin the kettle was to be
filled, Dinah came in—my Dinah—her sleeves rowled
up to the elbow an' her hair in a winkin' glory over
her forehead, the big blue eyes beneath twinklin' like
stars on a frosty night, an' the tread av her two feet
lighter than waste-paper from the Colonel's basket in
ord'ly-room whin ut's emptied.   Bein' but a shlip av
a girl she went pink at seein' me, an' I twisted me
moustache an' looked at a picture forninst the wall.
Niver show a woman that ye care the snap av a
finger for her, an' begad she'll come bleatin' to your
boot-heels ! '

'I suppose that's why you followed Annie Bragin
till everybody in the married quarters laughed at you,'
said I, remembering that unhallowed wooing and
casting off the disguise of drowsiness.

'I'm layin' down the gin'ral theory av the attack,'
said Mulvaney, driving his boot into the dying fire.
'If you read the *Soldier's Pocket-Book*, which niver
any soldier reads, you'll see that there are exceptions.
Whin Dinah was out av the door (an' 'twas as tho'
the sunlight had shut too)—"Mother av Hiven,
Sargint," sez I, "but is that your daughter ? "—" I've
believed that way these eighteen years," sez ould
Shadd, his eyes twinklin' ; "but Mrs. Shadd has her
own opinion, like iv'ry woman."—" 'Tis wid yours
this time, for a mericle," sez Mother Shadd.   "Thin
why in the name av fortune did I niver see her
before ? " sez I.   "Bekaze you've been thrapesin'
round wid the married women these three years past.
She was a bit av a child till last year, an' she shot
up wid the spring," sez ould Mother Shadd.   "I'll
thrapese no more," sez I   "D'you mane that ? " sez

' Thin whin the kettle was to be filled, Dinah came in—my Dinah.'—P. 100.

ould Mother Shadd, lookin' at me side-ways like a
hen looks at a hawk whin the chickens are runnin'
free. " Try me, an' tell," sez I. Wid that I pulled
on my gloves, dhrank off the tay, an' went out av the
house as stiff as at gin'ral p'rade, for well I knew that
Dinah Shadd's eyes were in the small av my back
out av the scullery window. Faith! that was the
only time I mourned I was not a cav'lry man for the
pride av the spurs to jingle.

'I wint out to think, an' I did a powerful lot av
thinkin', but ut all came round to that shlip av a girl
in the dotted blue dhress, wid the blue eyes an' the
sparkil in them. Thin I kept off canteen, an' I kept
to the married quarthers, or near by, on the chanst
av meetin' Dinah. Did I meet her? Oh, my time
past, did I not; wid a lump in my throat as big as
my valise an' my heart goin' like a farrier's forge on
a Saturday mornin? 'Twas "Good day to ye, Miss
Dinah," an' " Good day t'you, Corp'ril," for a week or
two, and divil a bit further could I get bekaze av the
respect I had to that girl that I cud ha' broken betune finger an' thumb.'

Here I giggled as I recalled the gigantic figure
of Dinah Shadd when she handed me my shirt.

'Ye may laugh,' grunted Mulvaney. 'But I'm
speakin' the trut', an' 'tis you that are in fault.
Dinah was a girl that wud ha' taken the imperious-
ness out av the Duchess av Clonmel in those days.
Flower hand, foot av shod air, an' the eyes av the
livin' mornin' she had that is my wife to-day—ould
Dinah, and niver aught else than Dinah Shadd to me.

' 'Twas after three weeks standin' off an' on, an'
niver makin' headway excipt through the eyes, that

a little drummer-boy grinned in me face whin I had
admonished him wid the buckle av my belt for
riotin' all over the place. " An' I'm not the only
wan that doesn't kape to barricks," sez he. I tuk
him by the scruff av his neck,—my heart was hung
on a hair-thrigger those days, you will onderstand—
an' " Out wid ut," sez I, " or I'll lave no bone av you
unbreakable."—" Speak to Dempsey," sez he howlin'.
" Dempsey which?" sez I, "ye unwashed limb av
Satan."—" Av the Bob-tailed Dhragoons," sez he.
" He's seen her home from her aunt's house in the
civil lines four times this fortnight."—" Child!" sez
I, dhroppin' him, "you're tongue's stronger than your
body. Go to your quarters. I'm sorry I dhressed
you down."

'At that I went four ways to wanst huntin'
Dempsey. I was mad to think that wid all my airs
among women I shud ha' been chated by a basin-
faced fool av a cav'lry-man not fit to trust on a
trunk. Presintly I found him in our lines—the
Bobtails was quartered next us — an' a tallowy,
topheavy son av a she-mule he was wid his big brass
spurs an' his plastrons on his epigastrons an' all.
But he niver flinched a hair.

' " A word wid you, Dempsey," sez I. " You've
walked wid Dinah Shadd four times this fortnight
gone."

' " What's that to you?" sez he. " I'll walk forty
times more, an' forty on top av that, ye shovel-futted
clod-breakin' infantry lance-corp'ril."

' Before I cud gyard he had his gloved fist home
on my cheek an' down I went full-sprawl. " Will
that content you?" sez he, blowin' on his knuckles

' "My collar-bone's bruk," sez he.'—P. 103.

for all the world like a Scots Greys orf'cer. "Content!" sez I. "For your own sake, man, take off
your spurs, peel your jackut, an' onglove. 'Tis the
beginnin' av the overture ; stand up ! "

'He stud all he know, but he niver peeled his
jacket, an' his shoulders had no fair play. I was
fightin' for Dinah Shadd an' that cut on my cheek.
What hope had he forninst me? "Stand up," sez
I, time an' again whin he was beginnin' to quarter
the ground an' gyard high an' go large. "This isn't
ridin'-school," I sez. "O man, stand up an' let me
get in at ye." But whin I saw he wud be runnin'
about, I grup his shtock in my left an' his waist-belt
in my right an' swung him clear to my right front,
head undher, he hammerin' my nose till the wind
was knocked out av him on the bare ground.
"Stand up," sez I, "or I'll kick your head into your
chest ! " and I wud ha' done ut too, so ragin' mad I
was.

'"My collar-bone's bruk," sez he. "Help me
back to lines. I'll walk wid her no more." So I
helped him back.'

'And was his collar-bone broken?' I asked, for I
fancied that only Learoyd could neatly accomplish
that terrible throw.

'He pitched on his left shoulder-point. Ut was.
Next day the news was in both barricks, an' whin I
met Dinah Shadd wid a cheek on me like all the
rig'mintal tailor's samples there was no "Good
mornin', Corp'ril," or aught else. "An' what have I
done, Miss Shadd," sez I, very bould, plantin' mesilf
forninst her, "that ye should not pass the time of
day ? "

' " Ye've half-killed rough-rider Dempsey," sez she, her dear blue eyes fillin' up.

' " Maybe," sez I. " Was he a friend av yours that saw ye home four times in the fortnight ? "

' " Yes," sez she, but her mouth was down at the corners. " An'—an' what's that to you ? " she sez.

' " Ask Dempsey," sez I, purtendin' to go away.

' " Did you fight for me then, ye silly man ? " she sez, tho' she knew ut all along.

' " Who else ? " sez I, an' I tuk wan pace to the front.

' " I wasn't worth ut," sez she, fingerin' in her apron.

' " That's for me to say," sez I. " Shall I say ut ? "

' " Yes," sez she in a saint's whisper, an' at that I explained mesilf; and she tould me what ivry man that is a man, an' many that is a woman, hears wanst in his life.

' " But what made ye cry at startin', Dinah, darlin' ? " sez I.

' " Your—your bloody cheek," sez she, duckin' her little head down on my sash (I was on duty for the day) an' whimperin' like a sorrowful angil.

' Now a man cud take that two ways. I tuk ut as pleased me best an' my first kiss wid ut. Mother av Innocence ! but I kissed her on the tip av the nose an' undher the eye ; an' a girl that lets a kiss come tumbleways like that has never been kissed before. Take note av that, Sorr. Thin we wint hand in hand to ould Mother Shadd like two little childher, an' she said 'twas no bad thing, an' ould Shadd nodded behind his pipe, an' Dinah ran away to her own room. That day I throd on rollin'

clouds. All earth was too small to hould me. Begad, I cud ha' hiked the sun out av the sky for a
live coal to my pipe, so magnificent I was. But I
tuk recruities at squad-drill instid, an' began wid
general battalion advance whin I shud ha' been
balance-steppin' them. Eyah! that day! that day!'
A very long pause. 'Well?' said I.

''Twas all wrong,' said Mulvaney, with an enor-
mous sigh. 'An' I know that iv'ry bit av ut was
my own foolishness. That night I tuk maybe the
half av three pints—not enough to turn the hair of
a man in his natural senses. But I was more than
half drunk wid pure joy, an' that canteen beer was
so much whisky to me. I can't tell how it came
about, but *bekaze* I had no thought for any wan
except Dinah, *bekaze* I hadn't slipped her little
white arms from my neck five minuts, *bekaze* the
breath of her kiss was not gone from my mouth, I
must go through the married lines on my way to
quarters an' I must stay talkin' to a red-headed
Mullingar heifer av a girl, Judy Sheehy, that was
daughter to Mother Sheehy, the wife of Nick Sheehy,
the canteen-sargint—the Black Curse av Shielygh
be on the whole brood that are above groun' this
day!

'"An' what are ye houldin' your head that high
for, Corp'ril?" sez Judy. "Come in an' thry a cup
av tay," she sez, standin' in the doorway. Bein' an on-
trustable fool, an' thinkin' av anything but tay, I wint.

'"Mother's at canteen," sez Judy, smoothin' the
hair av hers that was like red snakes, an' lookin' at
me corner-ways out av her green cats' eyes. "Ye
will not mind, Corp'ril?"

'"I can endure," sez I ; ould Mother Sheehy bein' no divarsion av mine, nor her daughter too. Judy fetched the tea things an' put thim on the table, leanin' over me very close to get thim square. I dhrew back, thinkin' av Dinah.

'"Is ut afraid you are av a girl alone ? " sez Judy.

'"No," sez I. "Why should I be ? "

'"That rests wid the girl," sez Judy, dhrawin' her chair next to mine.

'"Thin there let ut rest," sez I ; an' thinkin' I'd been a trifle onpolite, I sez, "The tay's not quite sweet enough for my taste. Put your little finger in the cup, Judy. 'Twill make ut necthar."

'"What's necthar ? " sez she.

'"Somethin' very sweet," sez I ; an' for the sinful life av me I cud not help lookin' at her out av the corner av my eye, as I was used to look at a woman.

'"Go on wid ye, Corp'ril," sez she. "You're a flirrt."

'"On me sowl I'm not," sez I.

'"Then you're a cruel handsome man, an' that's worse," sez she, heaving big sighs an' lookin' crossways.

'"You know your own mind," sez I.

'"'Twud be better for me if I did not," she sez.

'"There's a dale to be said on both sides av that," sez I, unthinkin'.

'"Say your own part av ut, then, Terence, darlin'," sez she ; "for begad I'm thinkin' I've said too much or too little for an honest girl," an' wid that she put her arms round my neck an' kissed me.

'"There's no more to be said afther that," sez I,

kissin' her back again—Oh the mane scutt that I was, my head ringin' wid Dinah Shadd! How does ut come about, Sorr, that when a man has put the comether on wan woman, he's sure bound to put it on another? 'Tis the same thing at musketry. Wan day iv'ry shot goes wide or into the bank, an' the next, lay high lay low, sight or snap, ye can't get off the bull's-eye for ten shots runnin'.'

'That only happens to a man who has had a good deal of experience. He does it without think-ing,' I replied.

'Thankin' you for the complimint, Sorr, ut may be so. But I'm doubtful whether you mint ut for a complimint. Hear now; I sat there wid Judy on my knee tellin' me all manner av nonsinse an' only sayin' "yes" an' "no," when I'd much better ha' kept tongue betune teeth. An' that was not an hour afther I had left Dinah! What I was thinkin' av I cannot say. Presintly, quiet as a cat, ould Mother Sheehy came in velvet-dhrunk. She had her daughter's red hair, but 'twas bald in patches, an' I could see in her wicked ould face, clear as lightnin', what Judy wud be twenty years to come. I was for jumpin' up, but Judy niver moved.

'"Terence has promust, mother," sez she, an' the could sweat bruk out all over me. Ould Mother Sheehy sat down of a heap an' began playin' wid the cups. "Thin you're a well-matched pair," she sez very thick. "For he's the biggest rogue that iver spoiled the Queen's shoe-leather, an'——"

'"I'm off, Judy," sez I. "Ye should not talk nonsinse to your mother. Get her to bed, girl."

'"Nonsinse!" sez the ould woman, prickin' up

her ears like a cat an' grippin' the table-edge.
" 'Twill be the most nonsinsical nonsinse for you, ye
grinnin' badger, if nonsinse 'tis. Git clear, you. I'm
goin' to bed."

'I ran out into the dhark, my head in a stew an'
my heart sick, but I had sinse enough to see that I'd
brought ut all on mysilf. " It's this to pass the time
av day to a panjandhrum av hell-cats," sez I. " What
I've said, an' what I've not said do not matther.
Judy an' her dam will hould me for a promust man,
an' Dinah will give me the go, an' I desarve ut. I
will go an' get dhrunk," sez I, " an' forget about ut,
for 'tis plain I'm not a marrin' man."

'On my way to canteen I ran against Lascelles,
Colour-Sargint that was av E Comp'ny, a hard, hard
man, wid a torment av a wife. " You've the head av
a drowned man on your shoulders," sez he ; " an'
you're goin' where you'll get a worse wan. Come
back," sez he. " Let me go," sez I. " I've thrown
my luck over the wall wid my own hand ! "—" Then
that's not the way to get ut back again," sez he.
" Have out wid your throuble, ye fool-bhoy." An'
I tould him how the matther was.

'He sucked in his lower lip. " You've been
thrapped," sez he. " Ju Shechy wud be the betther
for a man's name to hers as soon as can. An' ye
thought ye'd put the comether on her,—that's the
natural vanity of the baste. Terence, you're a big
born fool, but you're not bad enough to marry into
that comp'ny. If you said anythin', an' for all your
protestations I'm sure ye did—or did not, which is
worse,—eat ut all—lie like the father of all lies, but
come out av ut free av Judy. Do I not know what

ut is to marry a woman that was the very spit an' image av Judy whin she was young? I'm gettin' old an' I've larnt patience, but you, Terence, you'd raise hand on Judy an' kill her in a year. Never mind if Dinah gives you the go, you've desarved ut; never mind if the whole rig'mint laughs you all day. Get shut av Judy an' her mother. They can't dhrag you to church, but if they do, they'll dhrag you to hell. Go back to your quarters and lie down," sez he. Thin over his shoulder, "You *must* ha' done with thim."

'Next day I wint to see Dinah, but there was no tucker in me as I walked. I knew the throuble wud come soon enough widout any handlin' av mine, an' I dreaded ut sore.

'I heard Judy callin' me, but I hild straight on to the Shadds' quarthers, an' Dinah wud ha' kissed me but I put her back.

'"Whin all's said, darlin'," sez I, "you can give ut me if ye will, tho' I misdoubt 'twill be so easy to come by then."

'I had scarce begun to put the explanation into shape before Judy an' her mother came to the door. I think there was a veranda, but I'm forgettin'.

'"Will ye not step in?" sez Dinah, pretty and polite, though the Shadds had no dealin's with the Sheehys. Old Mother Shadd looked up quick, an' she was the fust to see the throuble; for Dinah was her daughter.

'"I'm pressed for time to-day," sez Judy as bould as brass; "an' I've only come for Terence,—my promust man. 'Tis strange to find him here the day afther the day."

'Dinah looked at me as though I had hit her, an' I answered straight.

'"There was some nonsinse last night at the Sheehys' quarthers, an' Judy's carryin' on the joke, darlin'," sez I.

'"At the Sheehys' quarthers?" sez Dinah very slow, an' Judy cut in wid: "He was there from nine till ten, Dinah Shadd, an' the betther half av that time I was sittin' on his knee, Dinah Shadd. Ye may look and ye may look an' ye may look me up an' down, but ye won't look away that Terence is my promust man. Terence, darlin', 'tis time for us to be comin' home."

'Dinah Shadd niver said word to Judy. "Ye left me at half-past eight," she sez to me, "an' I niver thought that ye'd leave me for Judy,—promises or no promises. Go back wid her, you that have to be fetched by a girl! I'm done with you," sez she, and she ran into her own room, her mother followin'. So I was alone wid those two women and at liberty to spake my sentiments.

'"Judy Sheehy," sez I, "if you made a fool av me betune the lights you shall not do ut in the day. I niver promised you words or lines."

'"You lie," sez ould Mother Sheehy, "an' may ut choke you where you stand!" She was far gone in dhrink.

'"An' tho' ut choked me where I stud I'd not change," sez I. "Go home, Judy. I take shame for a decent girl like you dhraggin' your mother out bareheaded on this errand. Hear now, and have ut for an answer. I gave my word to Dinah Shadd yesterday, an', more blame to me, I was wid you last

night talkin' nonsinse but nothin' more.   You've
chosen to thry to hould me on ut.   I will not be
held thereby for anythin' in the world.   Is that
enough ? "

'Judy wint pink all over.   " An' I wish you joy
av the perjury," sez she, duckin' a curtsey.   " You've
lost a woman that would ha' wore her hand to the
bone for your pleasure ; an' 'deed, Terence, ye were
not thrapped. . . ."   Lascelles must ha' spoken plain
to her.   " I am such as Dinah is—'deed I am !   Ye've
lost a fool av a girl that'll niver look at you again,
an' ye've lost what ye niver had—your common
honesty.   If you manage your men as you manage
your love-makin', small wondher they call you the
worst corp'ril in the comp'ny.   Come away, mother,"
sez she.

'But divil a fut would the ould woman budge !
" D'you hould by that ? " sez she, peerin' up under
her thick gray eyebrows.

'" Ay, an' wud," sez I, " tho' Dinah gave me the
go twenty times.   I'll have no thruck with you or
yours," sez I.   " Take your child away, ye shameless
woman."

'" An' am I shameless ? " sez she, bringin' her
hands up above her head.   " Thin what are you, ye
lyin', schamin', weak-kneed, dhirty-souled son av a
sutler ?   Am *I* shameless ?   Who put the open
shame on me an' my child that we shud go beggin'
through the lines in the broad daylight for the
broken word of a man ?   Double portion of my
shame be on you, Terence Mulvaney, that think
yourself so strong !   By Mary and the saints, by
blood and water an' by iv'ry sorrow that came into

the world since the beginnin', the black blight fall
on you and yours, so that you may niver be free
from pain for another when ut's not your own!
May your heart bleed in your breast drop by drop
wid all your friends laughin' at the bleedin'! Strong
you think yourself? May your strength be a curse
to you to dhrive you into the divil's hands against
your own will! Clear-eyed you are? May your
eyes see clear iv'ry step av the dark path you take
till the hot cindhers av hell put thim out! May the
ragin' dry thirst in my own ould bones go to you
that you shall niver pass bottle full nor glass empty.
God preserve the light av your onderstandin' to you,
my jewel av a bhoy, that ye may niver forget what
you mint to be an' do, whin you're wallowin' in the
muck! May ye see the betther and follow the
worse as long as there's breath in your body; an'
may ye die quick in a strange land, watchin' your
death before ut takes you, an' onable to stir hand or
foot!"

'I heard a scufflin' in the room behind, and thin
Dinah Shadd's hand dhropped into mine like a rose-
leaf into a muddy road.

'"The half av that I'll take," sez she, "an' more
too if I can. Go home, ye silly talkin' woman,—go
home an' confess."

'"Come away! Come away!" sez Judy, pullin'
her mother by the shawl. "'Twas none av Terence's
fault. For the love av Mary stop the talkin'!"

'"An' you!" said ould Mother Sheehy, spinnin'
round forninst Dinah. "Will ye take the half av
that man's load? Stand off from him, Dinah Shadd,
before he takes you down too—you that look to be a

' '' The half av that I'll take," sez she.'—P. 112.

quarther-master-ṣargint's wife in five ycars. You look too high, child. You shall *wash* for the quarther-master-sargint, whin he plases to give you the job out av charity ; but a privit's wife you shall be to the end, an' iv'ry sorrow of a privit's wife you shall know and niver a joy but wan, that shall go from you like the running tide from a rock. The pain av bearin' you shall know but niver the pleasure av giving the breast ; an' you shall put away a man-child into the common ground wid niver a priest to say a praycr over him, an' on that man-child ye shall think iv'ry day av your life. Think long, Dinah Shadd, for you'll niver have another tho' you pray till your knees are bleedin'. The mothers av childer shall mock you behind your back when you're wringing over the wash-tub. You shall know what ut is to hclp a dhrunken husband home an' see him go to the gyard-room. Will that plase you, Dinah Shadd, that won't be secn talkin' to my daughter ? You shall talk to worse than Judy before all's over. The sargints' wives shall look down on you contemptuous, daughter av a sargint, an' you shall cover ut all up wid a smiling face whin your heart's burstin'. Stand off av him, Dinah Shadd, for I've put the Black Curse of Shielygh upon him an' his own mouth shall make ut good."

' She pitchcd forward on her head an' began foamin' at the mouth. Dinah Shadd ran out wid water, an' Judy dhraggcd the ould woman into the veranda till she sat up.

' " I'm old an' forlore," she sez, thremblin' an' cryin', " and 'tis like I say a dale more than I mane."

I

' " When you're able to walk—go," says ould
Mother Shadd.   " This house has no place for the
likes av you that have cursed my daughter."

' " Eyah ! " said the ould woman.   " Hard words
break no bones, an' Dinah Shadd 'll kape the love av
her husband till my bones are green corn.   Judy,
darlin', I misremember what I came here for.   Can
you lend us the bottom av a taycup av tay, Mrs.
Shadd ? "

' But Judy dhragged her off cryin' as tho' her
heart wud break.   An' Dinah Shadd an' I, in ten
minutes we had forgot ut all.'

' Then why do you remember it now ? ' said I.

' Is ut like I'd forget?   Iv'ry word that wicked
ould woman spoke fell thrue in my life aftherwards,
an' I cud ha' stud ut all—stud ut all,—excipt when
my little Shadd was born.   That was on the line av
march three months afther the regiment was taken
with cholera.   We were betune Umballa an' Kalka
thin, an' I was on picket.   Whin I came off duty
the women showed me the child, an' ut turned on
uts side an' died as I looked.   We buried him by
the road, an' Father Victor was a day's march
behind wid the heavy baggage, so the comp'ny
captain read a prayer.   An' since then I've been a
childless man, an' all else that ould Mother Shechy
put upon me an' Dinah Shadd.   What do you
think, Sorr ? '

I thought a good deal, but it seemed better then
to reach out for Mulvaney's hand.   The demonstration nearly cost me the use of three fingers.   Whatever he knows of his weaknesses, Mulvaney is entirely
ignorant of his strength.

'But what do you think?' he repeated, as I was straightening out the crushed fingers.

My reply was drowned in yells and outcries from the next fire, where ten men were shouting for 'Orth'ris,' 'Privit Orth'ris,' 'Mistah Or—ther—ris!' 'Deah boy,' 'Cap'n Orth'ris,' 'Field-Marshal Orth'ris,' 'Stanley, you pen'north o' pop, come 'ere to your own comp'ny!' And the Cockney, who had been delighting another audience with recondite and Rabelaisian yarns, was shot down among his admirers by the major force.

'You've crumpled my dress-shirt 'orrid,' said he, 'an' I shan't sing no more to this 'ere bloomin' drawin'-room.'

Learoyd, roused by the confusion, uncoiled himself, crept behind Ortheris, and slung him aloft on his shoulders.

'Sing, ye bloomin' hummin' bird!' said he, and Ortheris, beating time on Learoyd's skull, delivered himself, in the raucous voice of the Ratcliffe Highway, of this song :—

> My girl she give me the go onst,
>   When I was a London lad,
> An' I went on the drink for a fortnight,
>   An' then I went to the bad.
> The Queen she give me a shillin'
>   To fight for 'er over the seas ;
> But Guv'ment built me a fever-trap,
>   An' Injia give me disease.
>
> *Chorus.*
>
> Ho! don't you 'eed what a girl says,
>   An' don't you go for the beer ;
> But I was an ass when I was at grass,
>   An' that is why I'm here.

I fired a shot at a Afghan,
    The beggar 'e fired again,
An' I lay on my bed with a 'ole in my 'ed,
    An' missed the next campaign !
I up with my gun at a Burman
    Who carried a bloomin' *dah*,
But the cartridge stuck and the bay'nit bruk,
    An' all I got was the scar.

Chorus.

Ho ! don't you aim at a Afghan
    When you stand on the sky-line clear ;
An' don't you go for a Burman
    If none o' your friends is near.

I served my time for a corp'ral,
    An' wetted my stripes with pop,
For I went on the bend with a intimate friend,
    An' finished the night in the ' shop.'
I served my time for a sergeant ;
    The colonel 'e sez ' No !
The most you'll see is a full C.B.' [1]
    An' . . . very next night 'twas so.

Chorus.

Ho ! don't you go for a corp'ral
    Unless your 'ed is clear ;
But I was an ass when I was at grass,
    An' that is why I'm 'ere.

I've tasted the luck o' the army
    In barrack an' camp an' clink,
An' I lost my tip through the bloomin' trip
    Along o' the women an' drink.
I'm down at the heel o' my service
    An' when I am laid on the shelf,
My very wust friend from beginning to end
    By the blood of a mouse was myself !

---

[1] Confined to barracks.

Chorus.

Ho! don't you 'eed what a girl says,
An' don't you go for the beer ;
But I was an ass when I was at grass,
An' that is why I'm 'ere.

'Ay, listen to our little man now, singin' an' shoutin' as tho' trouble had niver touched him. D' you remember when he went mad with the home-sickness?' said Mulvaney, recalling a never-to-be-forgotten season when Ortheris waded through the deep waters of affliction and behaved abominably. 'But he's talkin' bitter truth, though. Eyah!

'My very worst frind from beginnin' to ind
By the blood av a mouse was mesilf!'

.   .   .   .   .   .

When I woke I saw Mulvaney, the night-dew gemming his moustache, leaning on his rifle at picket, lonely as Prometheus on his rock, with I know not what vultures tearing his liver.

I

THE INCARNATION OF KRISHNA
MULVANEY

Wohl auf, my bully cavaliers
  We ride to church to-day,
The man that hasn't got a horse
  Must steal one straight away.

Be reverent, men, remember
  This is a Gottes haus.
Du, Conrad, cut along der aisle
  And schenck der whiskey aus.
              Hans Breitmann's Ride to Church.

ONCE upon a time, very far from England, there
lived three men who loved each other so greatly
that neither man nor woman could come between
them. They were in no sense refined, nor to be
admitted to the outer-door mats of decent folk,
because they happened to be private soldiers in
Her Majesty's Army ; and private soldiers of our
service have small time for self-culture. Their
duty is to keep themselves and their accoutrements
specklessly clean, to refrain from getting drunk more
often than is necessary, to obey their superiors, and
to pray for a war. All these things my friends
accomplished ; and of their own motion threw in
some fighting-work for which the Army Regulations

did not call. Their fate sent them to serve in India, which is not a golden country, though poets have sung otherwise. There men die with great swiftness, and those who live suffer many and curious things. I do not think that my friends concerned themselves much with the social or political aspects of the East. They attended a not unimportant war on the northern frontier, another one on our western boundary, and a third in Upper Burma. Then their regiment sat still to recruit, and the boundless monotony of cantonment life was their portion. They were drilled morning and evening on the same dusty parade-ground. They wandered up and down the same stretch of dusty white road, attended the same church and the same grog-shop, and slept in the same lime-washed barn of a barrack for two long years. There was Mulvaney, the father in the craft, who had served with various regiments from Bermuda to Halifax, old in war, scarred, reckless, resourceful, and in his pious hours an unequalled soldier. To him turned for help and comfort six and a half feet of slow-moving, heavy-footed Yorkshireman, born on the wolds, bred in the dales, and educated chiefly among the carriers' carts at the back of York railway-station. His name was Learoyd, and his chief virtue an unmitigated patience which helped him to win fights. How Ortheris, a foxterrier of a Cockney, ever came to be one of the trio, is a mystery which even to-day I cannot explain. ' There was always three av us,' Mulvaney used to say. ' An' by the grace av God, so long as our service lasts, three av us they'll always be. 'Tis betther so.'

They desired no companionship beyond their

own, and it was evil for any man of the regiment who attempted dispute with them. Physical argument was out of the question as regarded Mulvaney and the Yorkshireman; and assault on Ortheris meant a combined attack from these twain — a business which no five men were anxious to have on their hands. Therefore they flourished, sharing their drinks, their tobacco, and their money; good luck and evil; battle and the chances of death; life and the chances of happiness from Calicut in southern, to Peshawur in northern India.

Through no merit of my own it was my good fortune to be in a measure admitted to their friendship—frankly by Mulvaney from the beginning, sullenly and with reluctance by Learoyd, and suspiciously by Ortheris, who held to it that no man not in the Army could fraternise with a red-coat. 'Like to like,' said he. 'I'm a bloomin' sodger— he's a bloomin' civilian. 'Taint natural—that's all.'

But that was not all. They thawed progressively, and in the thawing told me more of their lives and adventures than I am ever likely to write.

Omitting all else, this tale begins with the Lamentable Thirst that was at the beginning of First Causes. Never was such a thirst—Mulvaney told me so. They kicked against their compulsory virtue, but the attempt was only successful in the case of Ortheris. He, whose talents were many, went forth into the highways and stole a dog from a 'civilian'—*videlicet*, some one, he knew not who, not in the Army. Now that civilian was but newly connected by marriage with the Colonel of the regiment, and outcry was made from quarters least anticipated by Ortheris, and, in the end, he was forced, lest a worse thing should happen, to dispose at ridiculously unremunerative rates of as promising a small terrier as ever graced one end of a leading string. The purchase-money was barely sufficient for one small outbreak which led him to the guard-room. He escaped, however, with nothing worse than a severe reprimand, and a few hours of punishment drill. Not for nothing had he acquired the reputation of being 'the best soldier of his inches' in the regiment. Mulvaney had taught personal cleanliness and efficiency as the first articles of his companions' creed. 'A dhirty man,' he was used to say, in the speech of his kind, 'goes to Clink for a weakness in the knees, an' is coort-martialled for a pair av socks missin'; but a clane man, such as is an ornament to his service—a man whose buttons are gold, whose coat is wax upon him, an' whose 'coutrements are widout a speck—*that* man may, spakin' in reason, do fwhat he likes an' dhrink from day to divil. That's the pride av bein' dacint.'

We sat together, upon a day, in the shade of a ravine far from the barracks, where a watercourse used to run in rainy weather. Behind us was the scrub jungle, in which jackals, peacocks, the gray wolves of the North-Western Provinces, and occasionally a tiger estrayed from Central India, were supposed to dwell. In front lay the cantonment, glaring white under a glaring sun ; and on either side ran the broad road that led to Delhi.

It was the scrub that suggested to my mind the wisdom of Mulvaney taking a day's leave and going upon a shooting-tour. The peacock is a holy bird throughout India, and he who slays one is in danger of being mobbed by the nearest villagers ; but on the last occasion that Mulvaney had gone forth, he had contrived, without in the least offending local religious susceptibilities, to return with six beautiful peacock skins which he sold to profit. It seemed just possible then——

'But fwhat manner av use is ut to me goin' out widout a dhrink? The ground's powdher-dhry underfoot, an' ut gets unto the throat fit to kill,' wailed Mulvaney, looking at me reproachfully. 'An' a peacock is not a bird you can catch the tail av onless ye run. Can a man run on wather—an' jungle-wather too?'

Ortheris had considered the question in all its bearings. He spoke, chewing his pipe-stem meditatively the while :

> 'Go forth, return in glory,
>   To Clusium's royal 'ome :
> An' round these bloomin' temples 'ang
>   The bloomin' shields o' Rome.

You better go. You ain't like to shoot yourself— not while there's a chanst of liquor. Me an' Learoyd 'll stay at 'ome an' keep shop—'case o' anythin' turnin' up. But you go out with a gas-pipe gun an' ketch the little peacockses or somethin'. You kin get one day's leave easy as winkin'. Go along an' get it, an' get peacockses or somethin'.'

'Jock,' said Mulvaney, turning to Learoyd, who was half asleep under the shadow of the bank. He roused slowly.

'Sitha, Mulvaaney, go,' said he.

And Mulvaney went ; cursing his allies with Irish fluency and barrack-room point.

'Take note,' said he, when he had won his holiday, and appeared dressed in his roughest clothes with the only other regimental fowling-piece in his hand. 'Take note, Jock, an' you, Orth'ris, I am goin' in the face av my own will—all for to please you. I misdoubt anythin' will come av permiscuous huntin' afther peacockses in a desolit lan' ; an' I know that I will lie down an' die wid thirrrst. Me catch peacockses for you, ye lazy scutts—an' be sacrificed by the peasanthry—Ugh ! '

He waved a huge paw and went away.

At twilight, long before the appointed hour, he returned empty-handed, much begrimed with dirt.

'Peacockses ? ' queried Ortheris from the safe rest of a barrack-room table whereon he was smoking cross-legged, Learoyd fast asleep on a bench.

'Jock,' said Mulvaney without answering, as he stirred up the sleeper. 'Jock, can ye fight ? Will ye fight ? '

Very slowly the meaning of the words communicated itself to the half-roused man. He understood—and again—what might these things mean ? Mulvaney was shaking him savagely. Meantime the men in the room howled with delight. There was war in the confederacy at last—war and the breaking of bonds.

Barrack-room etiquette is stringent. On the direct challenge must follow the direct reply. This is more binding than the ties of tried friendship. Once again Mulvaney repeated the question. Learoyd answered by the only means in his power, and

so swiftly that the Irishman had barely time to avoid
the blow. The laughter around increased. Learoyd
looked bewilderedly at his friend—himself as greatly
bewildered. Ortheris dropped from the table because his world was falling.

'Come outside,' said Mulvaney, and as the occupants of the barrack-room prepared joyously to follow,
he turned and said furiously, 'There will be no fight
this night—onless any wan av you is wishful to
assist. The man that does, follows on.'

No man moved. The three passed out into the
moonlight, Learoyd fumbling with the buttons of his
coat. The parade-ground was deserted except for
the scurrying jackals. Mulvaney's impetuous rush
carried his companions far into the open ere Learoyd
attempted to turn round and continue the discussion.

'Be still now. 'Twas my fault for beginnin'
things in the middle av an end, Jock. I should ha'
comminst wid an explanation ; but Jock, dear, on
your sowl are ye fit, think you, for the finest fight
that iver was—betther than fightin' me ? Considher
before ye answer.'

More than ever puzzled, Learoyd turned round
two or three times, felt an arm, kicked tentatively,
and answered, 'Ah'm fit.' He was accustomed to
fight blindly at the bidding of the superior mind.

They sat them down, the men looking on from afar,
and Mulvaney untangled himself in mighty words.

'Followin' your fools' scheme I wint out into the
thrackless desert beyond the barricks. An' there I
met a pious Hindu dhriving a bullock-kyart. I tuk
ut for granted he wud be delighted for to convoy me
a piece, an' I jumped in——'

'You long, lazy, black-haired swine,' drawled Ortheris, who would have done the same thing under similar circumstances.

''Twas the height av policy. That naygur-man dhruv miles an' miles—as far as the new railway line they're buildin' now back av the Tavi river. "'Tis a kyart for dhirt only," says he now an' again timoreously, to get me out av ut. "Dhirt I am," sez I, "an' the dhryest that you iver kyarted. Dhrive on, me son, an' glory be wid you." At that I wint to slape, an' took no heed till he pulled up on the embankmint av the line where the coolies were pilin' mud. There was a matther av two thousand coolies on that line—you remimber that. Prisintly a bell rang, an' they throops off to a big pay-shed. "Where's the white man in charge?" sez I to my kyart-dhriver. "In the shed," sez he, "engaged on a riffle."—"A fwhat?" sez I. "Riffle," sez he. "You take ticket. He take money. You get nothin'."—"Oho!" sez I, "that's fwhat the shuperior an' cultivated man calls a raffle, me misbeguided child av darkness an' sin. Lead on to that raffle, though fwhat the mischief 'tis doin' so far away from uts home—which is the charity-bazaar at Christmas, an' the Colonel's wife grinnin' behind the tea-table—is more than I know." Wid that I wint to the shed an' found 'twas pay-day among the coolies. Their wages was on a table forninst a big, fine, red buck av a man—sivun fut high, four fut wide, an' three fut thick, wid a fist on him like a corn-sack. He was payin' the coolies fair an' easy, but he wud ask each man if he wud raffle that month, an' each man sez, "Yes," av course. Thin he wud deduct from their wages accordin'.

Whin all was paid, he filled an ould cigar-box full av gun-wads an' scatthered ut among the coolies. They did not take much joy av that performince, an' small wondher. A man close to me picks up a black gun-wad an' sings out, " I have ut."—" Good may ut do you," sez I. The coolie wint forward to this big, fine, red man, who threw a cloth off av the most sump-shus, jooled, enamelled an' variously bedivilled sedan-chair I iver saw.'

'Sedan-chair! Put your 'cad in a bag. That was a palanquin. Don't yer know a palanquin when you see it?' said Ortheris with great scorn.

'I chuse to call ut sedan-chair, an' chair ut shall be, little man,' continued the Irishman. ''Twas a most amazin' chair—all lined wid pink silk an' fitted wid red silk curtains. " Here ut is," sez the red man. " Here ut is," sez the coolie, an' he grinned weakly-ways. " Is ut any use to you?" sez the red man. " No," sez the coolie; "I'd like to make a presint av ut to you."—" I am graciously pleased to accept that same," sez the red man ; an' at that all the coolies cried aloud in fwhat was mint for cheer-ful notes, an' wint back to their diggin', lavin' me alone in the shed. The red man saw me, an' his face grew blue on his big, fat neck. " Fwhat d'you want here?" sez he. " Standin'-room an' no more," sez I, "onless it may be fwhat ye niver had, an' that's manners, ye rafflin' ruffian," for I was not goin' to have the Service throd upon. " Out of this," sez he. " I'm in charge av this section av construction." —" I'm in charge av mesilf," sez I, "an' it's like I will stay a while. D'ye raffle much in these parts?" —" Fwhat's that to you?" sez he. " Nothin'," sez I,

' "Out of this," sez he. " I'm in charge av this section av construction."—
" I'm in charge av mesilf," sez I, "an' it's like I will stay a while." '—P. 126.

" but a great dale to you, for begad I'm thinkin' you get the full half av your revenue from that sedan-chair. Is ut always raffled so ? " I sez, an' wid that I wint to a coolie to ask questions. Bhoys, that man's name is Dearsley, an' he's been rafflin' that ould sedan-chair monthly this matther av nine months. Iv'ry coolie on the section takes a ticket—or he gives 'em the go—wanst a month on pay-day. Iv'ry coolie that wins ut gives ut back to him, for 'tis too big to carry away, an' he'd sack the man that thried to sell ut. That Dearsley has been makin' the rowlin' wealth av Roshus by nefarious rafflin'. Think av the burnin' shame to the sufferin' coolie-man that the army in Injia are bound to protect an' nourish in their bosoms ! Two thousand coolies defrauded wanst a month ! '

' Dom t' coolies. Has't gotten t' cheer, man ? ' said Learoyd.

' Hould on. Havin' onearthed this amazin' an' stupenjus fraud committed by the man Dearsley, I hild a council av war ; he thryin' all the time to sejuce me into a fight wid opprobrious language. That sedan-chair niver belonged by right to any foreman av coolies. 'Tis a king's chair or a quane's. There's gold on ut an' silk an' all manner av trapese-mints. Bhoys, 'tis not for me to countenance any sort av wrong-doin'—me bein' the ould man—but ——anyway he has had ut nine months, an' he dare not make throuble av ut was taken from him. Five miles away, or ut may be six—— '

There was a long pause, and the jackals howled merrily. Learoyd bared one arm, and contemplated it in the moonlight. Then he nodded partly to himself and partly to his friends. Ortheris wriggled with suppressed emotion.

'I thought ye wud see the reasonableness av ut,' said Mulvaney. 'I made bould to say as much to the man before. He was for a direct front attack—fut, horse, an' guns——an' all for nothin', seein' that I had no thransport to convey the machine away. "I will not argue wid you," sez I, "this day, but subsequintly, Mister Dearsley, me rafflin' jool, we talk ut out lengthways. 'Tis no good policy to swindle the naygur av his hard-earned emolumints, an' by presint informashin"—'twas the kyart man that tould me—"ye've been perpethrating that same for nine months. But I'm a just man," sez I, "an' overlookin' the presumpshin that yondher settee wid the gilt top was not come by honust,"—at that he turned sky-green, so I knew things was more thrue than tellable—"not come by honust, I'm willin' to compound the felony for this month's winnin's."'

'Ah! Ho!' from Learoyd and Ortheris.

'That man Dearsley's rushin' on his fate,' continued Mulvaney, solemnly wagging his head. 'All Hell had no name bad enough for me that tide. Faith, he called me a robber! Me! that was savin' him from continuin' in his evil ways widout a remonstrince—an' to a man av conscience a remonstrince may change the chune av his life. "'Tis not for me to argue," sez I, "fwhatever ye are, Mister Dearsley, but, by my hand, I'll take away the temptation for you that lies in that sedan-chair."— "You will have to fight me for ut," sez he, "for well I know you will never dare make report to any one."—"Fight I will," sez I, "but not this day, for

I'm rejuced for want av nourishmint."—"Ye're an
ould bould hand," sez he, sizin' me up an' down ; "an'
a jool av a fight we will have.   Eat now an' dhrink,
an' go your way."   Wid that he gave me some hump
an' whisky—good whisky—an' we talked av this an'
that the while.   "It goes hard on me now," sez I,
wipin' my mouth, "to confiscate that piece av furni-
ture, but justice is justice."—"Ye've not got ut yet,"
sez he ; "there's the fight between."—"There is,"
sez I, "an' a good fight.   Ye shall have the pick av
the best quality in my rig'mint for the dinner you
have given this day."   Thin I came hot-foot to you
two.   Hould your tongue, the both.   'Tis this way.
To-morrow we three will go there an' he shall have
his pick betune me an' Jock.   Jock's a deceivin'
fighter, for he is all fat to the eye, an' he moves
slow.   Now I'm all beef to the look, an' I move
quick.   By my reckonin' the Dearsley man won't
take me ; so me an' Orth'ris 'll see fair play.   Jock,
I tell you, 'twill be big fightin'—whipped, wid the
cream above the jam.   Afther the business 'twill take
a good three av us—Jock 'll be very hurt—to haul
away that sedan-chair.'

'Palanquin.'   This from Ortheris.

'Fwhatever ut is, we must have ut.   'Tis the
only sellin' piece av property widin reach that we
can get so cheap.   An' fwhat's a fight afther all ?
He has robbed the naygur-man, dishonust.   We rob
him honust for the sake av the whisky he gave me.'

'But wot'll we do with the bloomin' article when
we've got it ?   Them palanquins are as big as
'ouses, an' uncommon 'ard to sell, as M'Cleary said
when ye stole the sentry-box from the Curragh.'

'Who's goin' to do t' fightin'?' said Learoyd, and
Ortheris subsided. The three returned to barracks
without a word. Mulvaney's last argument clinched
the matter. This palanquin was property, vendible
and to be attained in the simplest and least embar-
rassing fashion. It would eventually become beer.
Great was Mulvaney.

Next afternoon a procession of three formed
itself and disappeared into the scrub in the direction
of the new railway line. Learoyd alone was without
care, for Mulvaney dived darkly into the future, and
little Ortheris feared the unknown. What befell at
that interview in the lonely pay-shed by the side of
the half-built embankment, only a few hundred
coolies know, and their tale is a confusing one,
running thus—

'We were at work. Three men in red coats
came. They saw the Sahib — Dearsley Sahib.
They made oration; and noticeably the small man
among the red-coats. Dearsley Sahib also made
oration, and used many very strong words. Upon
this talk they departed together to an open space,
and there the fat man in the red coat fought with
Dearsley Sahib after the custom of white men—
with his hands, making no noise, and never at all
pulling Dearsley Sahib's hair. Such of us as were
not afraid beheld these things for just so long a time
as a man needs to cook the mid-day meal. The
small man in the red coat had possessed himself of
Dearsley Sahib's watch. No, he did not steal that
watch. He held it in his hand, and at certain
seasons made outcry, and the twain ceased their
combat, which was like the combat of young bulls in

spring. Both men were soon all red, but Dearsley
Sahib was much more red than the other. Seeing
this, and fearing for his life—because we greatly
loved him—some fifty of us made shift to rush upon
the red-coats. But a certain man—very black as to
the hair, and in no way to be confused with the
small man, or the fat man who fought—that man,
we affirm, ran upon us, and of us he embraced some
ten or fifty in both arms, and beat our heads
together, so that our livers turned to water, and we
ran away. It is not good to interfere in the fight-
ings of white men. After that Dearsley Sahib fell
and did not rise, these men jumped upon his
stomach and despoiled him of all his money, and
attempted to fire the pay-shed, and departed. Is it
true that Dearsley Sahib makes no complaint of
these latter things having been done? We were
senseless with fear, and do not at all remember.
There was no palanquin near the pay-shed. What
do we know about palanquins? Is it true that
Dearsley Sahib does not return to this place, on
account of his sickness, for ten days? This is the
fault of those bad men in the red coats, who should
be severely punished; for Dearsley Sahib is both
our father and mother, and we love him much. Yet,
if Dearsley Sahib does not return to this place at
all, we will speak the truth. There was a palanquin,
for the up-keep of which we were forced to pay nine-
tenths of our monthly wage. On such mulctings
Dearsley Sahib allowed us to make obeisance to him
before the palanquin. What could we do? We
were poor men. He took a full half of our wages.
Will the Government repay us those moneys?

Those three men in red coats bore the palanquin
upon their shoulders and departed. All the money
that Dearsley Sahib had taken from us was in the
cushions of that palanquin. Therefore they stole it.
Thousands of rupees were there—all our money.
It was our bank-box, to fill which we cheerfully con-
tributed to Dearsley, Sahib three-sevenths of our
monthly wage. Why does the white man look upon
us with the eye of disfavour? Before God, there
was a palanquin, and now there is no palanquin;
and if they send the police here to make inquisition,
we can only say that there never has been any
palanquin. Why should a palanquin be near these
works? We are poor men, and we know nothing.'

Such is the simplest version of the simplest story
connected with the descent upon Dearsley. From
the lips of the coolies I received it. Dearsley himself
was in no condition to say anything, and Mulvaney
preserved a massive silence, broken only by the
occasional licking of the lips. He had seen a fight
so gorgeous that even his power of speech was taken
from him. I respected that reserve until, three days
after the affair, I discovered in a disused stable in
my quarters a palanquin of unchastened splendour
—evidently in past days the litter of a queen. The
pole whereby it swung between the shoulders of the
bearers was rich with the painted *papier-maché* of
Cashmere. The shoulder-pads were of yellow silk.
The panels of the litter itself were ablaze with the
loves of all the gods and goddesses of the Hindu
Pantheon—lacquer on cedar. The cedar sliding
doors were fitted with hasps of translucent Jaipur
enamel and ran in grooves shod with silver. The

'Nine roun's they were even matched, an' at the tenth ——.'—P. 133.

cushions were of brocaded Delhi silk, and the curtains which once hid any glimpse of the beauty of the king's palace were stiff with gold. Closer investigation showed that the entire fabric was everywhere rubbed and discoloured by time and wear ; but even thus it was sufficiently gorgeous to deserve housing on the threshold of a royal zenana. I found no fault with it, except that it was in my stable. Then, trying to lift it by the silver-shod shoulder-pole, I laughed. The road from Dearsley's pay-shed to the cantonment was a narrow and uneven one, and, traversed by three very inexperienced palanquin-bearers, one of whom was sorely battered about the head, must have been a path of torment. Still I did not quite recognise the right of the three musketeers to turn me into a 'fence' for stolen property.

'I'm askin' you to warehouse ut,' said Mulvaney, when he was brought to consider the question. 'There's no steal in ut. Dearsley tould us we cud have ut if we fought. Jock fought—an', oh, Sorr, when the throuble was at uts finest an' Jock was bleedin' like a stuck pig, an' little Orth'ris was shqualin' on one leg chewin' big bites out' av Dearsley's watch, I wud ha' given my place at the fight to have had you see wan round. He tuk Jock, as I suspicioned he would, an' Jock was deceptive. Nine roun's they were even matched, an' at the tenth—— About that palanquin now. There's not the least throuble in the world, or we wud not ha' brought ut here. You will ondherstand that the Queen—God bless her !—does not reckon for a privit soldier to kape elephints an' palanquins an' sich in barricks. Afther we had dhragged ut down from Dearsley's through that cruel scrub that near broke Orth'ris's heart, we set ut in the ravine for a night ; an' a thief av a porcupine an' a civet-cat av a jackal roosted in ut, as well we knew in the mornin'. I put ut to you, Sorr, is an elegint palan-quin, fit for the princess, the natural abidin' place av all the vermin in cantonmints ? We brought ut to you, afther dhark, and put ut in your shtable. Do not let your conscience prick. Think av the rejoicin' men in the pay-shed yonder—lookin' at Dearsley wid his head tied up in a towel—an' well knowin' that they can dhraw their pay iv'ry month widout stoppages for riffles. Indirectly, Sorr, you have rescued from an onprincipled son av a night-hawk the peasanthry av a numerous village. An' besides, will I let that sedan-chair rot on our hands ? Not I. 'Tis not every day a piece av pure joolry comes into the market. There's not a king widin these forty miles '—he waved his hand round the dusty horizon—' not a king wud not be glad to buy ut. Some day mesilf, whin I have leisure, I'll take ut up along the road an' dishpose av ut.'

' How ? ' said I, for I knew the man was capable of anything.

' Get into ut, av coorse, and keep wan eye open through the curtains. Whin I see a likely man av the native persuasion, I will descind blushin' from my canopy and say, " Buy a palanquin, ye black scutt ? " I will have to hire four men to carry me first, though ; and that's impossible till next pay-day.'

Curiously enough, Learoyd, who had fought for

the prize, and in the winning secured the highest pleasure life had to offer him, was altogether disposed to undervalue it, while Ortheris openly said it would be better to break the thing up. Dearsley, he argued, might be a many-sided man, capable, despite his magnificent fighting qualities, of setting in motion the machinery of the civil law — a thing much abhorred by the soldier. Under any circumstances their fun had come and passed; the next pay-day was close at hand, when there would be beer for all. Wherefore longer conserve the painted palanquin?

'A first-class rifle-shot an' a good little man av your inches you are,' said Mulvaney. 'But you niver had a head worth a soft-boiled egg. 'Tis me has to lie awake av nights schamin' an' plottin' for the three av us. Orth'ris, me son, 'tis no matther av a few gallons av beer—no, nor twenty gallons— but tubs an' vats an' firkins in that sedan-chair. Who ut was, an' what ut was, an' how ut got there, we do not know; but I know in my bones that you an' me an' Jock wid his sprained thumb will get a fortune thereby. Lave me alone, an' let me think.'

Meantime the palanquin stayed in my stall, the key of which was in Mulvaney's hands.

Pay-day came, and with it beer. It was not in experience to hope that Mulvaney, dried by four weeks' drought, would avoid excess. Next morning he and the palanquin had disappeared. He had taken the precaution of getting three days' leave 'to see a friend on the railway,' and the Colonel, well knowing that the seasonal outburst was near, and hoping it would spend its force beyond the limits of his jurisdiction, cheerfully gave him all he demanded.

At this point Mulvaney's history, as recorded in the mess-room, stopped.

Ortheris carried it not much further. 'No, 'e wasn't drunk,' said the little man loyally, 'the liquor was no more than feelin' its way round inside of 'im ; but 'e went an' filled that 'ole bloomin' palanquin with bottles 'fore 'e went off. 'E's gone an' 'ired six men to carry 'im, an' I 'ad to 'elp 'im into 'is nupshal couch, 'cause 'e wouldn't 'ear reason. 'E's gone off in 'is shirt an' trousies, swearin' tremenjus—gone down the road in the palanquin, wavin' 'is legs out o' windy.'

'Yes,' said I, 'but where?'

'Now you arx me a question. 'E said 'e was goin' to sell that palanquin, but from observations what happened when I was stuffin' 'im through the door, I fancy 'e's gone to the new embankment to mock at Dearsley. 'Soon as Jock's off duty I'm goin' there to see if 'e's safe—not Mulvaney, but t'other man. My saints, but I pity 'im as 'elps Terence out o' the palanquin when 'e's once fair drunk ! '

'He'll come back without harm,' I said.

''Corse 'e will. On'y question is, what 'll 'e be doin' on the road? Killing Dearsley, like as not. 'E shouldn't 'a gone without Jock or me.'

Reinforced by Learoyd, Ortheris sought the foreman of the coolie-gang. Dearsley's head was still embellished with towels. Mulvaney, drunk or sober, would have struck no man in that condition, and Dearsley indignantly denied that he would have taken advantage of the intoxicated brave.

'I had my pick o' you two,' he explained to

Learoyd, 'and you got my palanquin—not before
I'd made my profit on it.   Why'd I do harm when
everything's settled?'   Your man *did* come here—
drunk as Davy's sow on a frosty night—came
a-purpose to mock me—stuck his head out of the
door an' called me a crucified hodman.   I made him
drunker, an' sent him along.   But I never touched
him.'

To these things Learoyd, slow to perceive the
evidences of sincerity, answered only, 'If owt comes
to Mulvaaney 'long o' you, I'll gripple you, clouts or
no clouts on your ugly head, an' I'll draw t' throat
twistyways, man.   See there now.'

The embassy removed itself, and Dearsley, the
battered, laughed alone over his supper that evening.

Three days passed—a fourth and a fifth.   The
week drew to a close and Mulvaney did not return.
He, his royal palanquin, and his six attendants, had
vanished into air.   A very large and very tipsy
soldier, his feet sticking out of the litter of a reigning
princess, is not a thing to travel along the ways without comment.   Yet no man of all the country round
had seen any such wonder.   He was, and he was
not ; and Learoyd suggested the immediate smash-
ment of Dearsley as a sacrifice to his ghost.   Ortheris
insisted that all was well, and in the light of past
experience his hopes seemed reasonable.

'When Mulvaney goes up the road,' said he, ''e's
like to go a very long ways up, specially when 'e's
so blue drunk as 'e is now.   But what gits me is 'is
not bein' 'eard of pullin' wool off the niggers somewheres about.   That don't look good.   The drink
must ha' died out in 'im by this, unless 'e's broke a

bank, an' then — Why don't 'e come back? 'E didn't ought to ha' gone off without us.'

Even Ortheris's heart sank at the end of the seventh day, for half the regiment were out scouring the countryside, and Learoyd had been forced to fight two men who hinted openly that Mulvaney had deserted. To do him justice, the Colonel laughed at the notion, even when it was put forward by his much-trusted Adjutant.

'Mulvaney would as soon think of deserting as you would,' said he. 'No; he's either fallen into a mischief among the villagers — and yet that isn't likely, for he'd blarney himself out of the Pit; or else he is engaged on urgent private affairs — some stupendous devilment that we shall hear of at mess after it has been the round of the barrack-rooms. The worst of it is that I shall have to give him twenty-eight days' confinement at least for being absent without leave, just when I most want him to lick the new batch of recruits into shape. I never knew a man who could put a polish on young soldiers as quickly as Mulvaney can. How does he do it?'

'With blarney and the buckle-end of a belt, Sir,' said the Adjutant. 'He is worth a couple of non-commissioned officers when we are dealing with an Irish draft, and the London lads seem to adore him. The worst of it is that if he goes to the cells the other two are neither to hold nor to bind till he comes out again. I believe Ortheris preaches mutiny on those occasions, and I know that the mere presence of Learoyd mourning for Mulvaney kills all the cheerfulness of his room. The sergeants tell me

that he allows no man to laugh when he feels un-
happy. They are a queer gang.'

'For all that, I wish we had a few more of them.
I like a well-conducted regiment, but these pasty-
faced, shifty-eyed, mealy-mouthed young slouchers
from the Depot worry me sometimes with their
offensive virtue. They don't seem to have backbone enough to do anything but play cards and
prowl round the married quarters. I believe I'd
forgive that old villain on the spot if he turned up
with any sort of explanation that I could in decency
accept.'

'Not likely to be much difficulty about that, Sir,'
said the Adjutant. 'Mulvaney's explanations are
only one degree less wonderful than his performances.
They say that when he was in the Black Tyrone,
before he came to us, he was discovered on the
banks of the Liffey trying to sell his colonel's
charger to a Donegal dealer as a perfect lady's hack.
Shackbolt commanded the Tyrone then.'

'Shackbolt must have had apoplexy at the
thought of his ramping war-horses answering to that
description. He used to buy unbacked devils, and
tame them on some pet theory of starvation. What
did Mulvaney say?'

'That he was a member of the Society for the
Prevention of Cruelty to Animals, anxious to "sell
the poor baste where he would get something to fill
out his dimples." Shackbolt laughed, but I fancy
that was why Mulvaney exchanged to ours.'

'I wish he were back,' said the Colonel; 'for I
like him and believe he likes me.'

That evening, to cheer our souls, Learoyd,

Ortheris, and I went into the waste to smoke out a porcupine. All the dogs attended, but even their clamour — and they began to discuss the short-comings of porcupines before they left cantonments —could not take us out of ourselves. A large, low moon turned the tops of the plume-grass to silver, and the stunted camelthorn bushes and sour tamarisks into the likenesses of trooping devils. The smell of the sun had not left the earth, and little aimless winds blowing across the rose-gardens to the south-ward brought the scent of dried roses and water. Our fire once started, and the dogs craftily disposed to wait the dash of the porcupine, we climbed to the top of a rain-scarred hillock of earth, and looked across the scrub seamed with cattle paths, white with the long grass, and dotted with spots of level pond-bottom, where the snipe would gather in winter.

'This,' said Ortheris, with a sigh, as he took in the unkempt desolation of it all, 'this is sanguinary. This is unusually sanguinary. Sort o' mad country. Like a grate when the fire's put out by the sun.' He shaded his eyes against the moonlight. 'An' there's a loony dancin' in the middle of it all. Quite right. I'd dance too if I wasn't so downheart.'

There pranced a Portent in the face of the moon —a huge and ragged spirit of the waste, that flapped its wings from afar. It had risen out of the earth ; it was coming towards us, and its outline was never twice the same. The toga, table-cloth, or dressing-gown, whatever the creature wore, took a hundred shapes. Once it stopped on a neighbouring mound and flung all its legs and arms to the winds.

'My, but that scarecrow 'as got 'em bad !' said

There pranced a Portent in the face of the moon. —P. 140.

Ortheris. 'Seems like if 'e comes any furder we'll 'ave to argify with 'im.'

Learoyd raised himself from the dirt as a bull clears his flanks of the wallow. And as a bull bellows, so he, after a short minute at gaze, gave tongue to the stars.

'MULVAANEY! MULVAANEY! A-hoo!'

Oh then it was that we yelled, and the figure dipped into the hollow, till, with a crash of rending grass, the lost one strode up to the light of the fire, and disappeared to the waist in a wave of joyous dogs! Then Learoyd and Ortheris gave greeting, bass and falsetto together, both swallowing a lump in the throat.

'You damned fool!' said they, and severally pounded him with their fists.

'Go easy!' he answered; wrapping a huge arm round each. 'I would have you to know that I am a god, to be treated as such—tho', by my faith, I fancy I've got to go to the guard-room just like a privit soldier.'

The latter part of the sentence destroyed the suspicions raised by the former. Any one would have been justified in regarding Mulvaney as mad. He was hatless and shoeless, and his shirt and trousers were dropping off him. But he wore one wondrous garment—a gigantic cloak that fell from collar-bone to heel—of pale pink silk, wrought all over in cunningest needlework of hands long since dead, with the loves of the Hindu gods. The monstrous figures leaped in and out of the light of the fire as he settled the folds round him.

Ortheris handled the stuff respectfully for a

moment while I was trying to remember where I had seen it before. Then he screamed, 'What 'ave you done with the palanquin? You're wearin' the linin'.'

'I am,' said the Irishman, 'an' by the same token the 'broidery is scrapin' my hide off. I've lived in this sumpshus counterpane for four days. Me son, I begin to ondherstand why the naygur is no use. Widout me boots, an' me trousies like an openwork stocking on a gyurl's leg at a dance, I begin to feel like a naygur-man—all fearful an' timoreous. Give me a pipe an' I'll tell on.'

He lit a pipe, resumed his grip of his two friends, and rocked to and fro in a gale of laughter.

'Mulvaney,' said Ortheris sternly, ''taint no time for laughin'. You've given Jock an' me more trouble than you're worth. You 'ave been absent without leave an' you'll go into cells for that; an' you 'ave come back disgustin'ly dressed an' most improper in the linin' o' that bloomin' palanquin. Instid of which you laugh. An' *we* thought you was dead all the time.'

'Bhoys,' said the culprit, still shaking gently, 'whin I've done my tale you may cry if you like, an' little Orth'ris here can thrample my inside out. Ha' done an' listen. My performinces have been stupenjus: my luck has been the blessed luck av the British Army—an' there's no betther than that. I went out dhrunk an' dhrinkin' in the palanquin, and I have come back a pink god. Did any of you go to Dearsley afther my time was up? He was at the bottom of ut all.'

'Ah said so,' murmured Learoyd. 'To-morrow ah'll smash t' face in upon his heead.'

'Ye will not. Dearsley's a jool av a man. Afther Ortheris had put me into the palanquin an' the six bearer-men were gruntin' down the road, I tuk thought to mock Dearsley for that fight. So I tould thim, "Go to the embankmint," and there, bein' most amazin' full, I shtuck my head out av the concern an' passed compliments wid Dearsley. I must ha' miscalled him outrageous, for whin I am that way the power av the tongue comes on me. I can bare remimber tellin' him that his mouth opened endways like the mouth av a skate, which was thrue afther Learoyd had handled ut; an' I clear remimber his takin' no manner nor matter av offence, but givin' me a big dhrink of beer. 'Twas the beer did the thrick, for I crawled back into the palanquin, steppin' on me right ear wid me left foot, an' thin I slept like the dead. Wanst I half-roused, an' begad the noise in my head was tremenjus— roarin' and rattlin' an' poundin', such as was quite new to me. "Mother av Mercy," thinks I, "phwat a concertina I will have on my shoulders whin I wake!" An' wid that I curls mysilf up to sleep before ut should get hould on me. Bhoys, that noise was not dhrink, 'twas the rattle av a thrain!'

There followed an impressive pause.

'Yes, he had put me on a thrain—put me, palanquin an' all, an' six black assassins av his own coolies that was in his nefarious confidence, on the flat av a ballast-thruck, and we were rowlin' an' bowlin' along to Benares. Glory be that I did not wake up thin an' introjuce mysilf to the coolies. As I was sayin', I slept for the betther part av a day an' a night. But remimber you, that that man Dearsley had

packed me off on wan av his material-thrains to
Benares, all for to make me overstay my leave an'
get me into the cells.'

The explanation was an eminently rational one.
Benares lay at least ten hours by rail from the
cantonments, and nothing in the world could have
saved Mulvaney from arrest as a deserter had he
appeared there in the apparel of his orgies. Dearsley had not forgotten to take revenge. Learoyd,
drawing back a little, began to play soft blows over
selected portions of Mulvaney's body. His thoughts
were away on the embankment, and they meditated
evil for Dearsley. Mulvaney continued—

'Whin I was full awake the palanquin was set
down in a street, I suspicioned, for I cud hear people
passin' an' talkin'. But I knew well I was far from
home. There is a queer smell upon our cantonments
—a smell av dried earth and brick-kilns wid whiffs
av cavalry stable-litter. This place smelt marigold
flowers an' bad water, an' wanst somethin' alive came
an' blew heavy with his muzzle at the chink av the
shutter. "It's in a village I am," thinks I to mysilf,
"an' the parochial buffalo is investigatin' the palanquin." But anyways I had no desire to move.
Only lie still whin you're in foreign parts an' the
standin' luck av the British Army will carry ye
through. That is an epigram. I made ut.

'Thin a lot av whishperin' divils surrounded the
palanquin. "Take ut up," sez wan man. "But
who'll pay us?" sez another. "The Maharanee's
minister, av coorse," sez the man. "Oho!" sez I
to mysilf, "I'm a quane in me own right, wid a
minister to pay me expenses. I'll be an emperor

if I lie still long enough ; but this is no village I've found." I lay quiet, but I gummed me right eye to a crack av the shutters, an' I saw that the whole street was crammed wid palanquins an' horses, an' a sprinklin' av naked priests all yellow powder an' tigers' tails. But I may tell you, Orth'ris, an' you, Learoyd, that av all the palanquins ours was the most imperial an' magnificent. Now a palanquin means a native lady all the world over, except whin a soldier av the Quane happens to be takin' a ride. " Women an' priests ! " sez I. " Your father's son is in the right pew this time, Terence. There will be proceedin's." Six black divils in pink muslin tuk up the palanquin, an' oh ! but the rowlin' an' the rockin' made me sick. Thin we got fair jammed among the palanquins—not more than fifty av them—an' we grated an' bumped like Queenstown potato-smacks in a runnin' tide. I cud hear the women gigglin' and squirkin' in their palanquins, but mine was the royal equipage. They made way for ut, an', begad, the pink muslin men o' mine were howlin', " Room for the Maharanee av Gokral-Seetarun." Do you know aught av the lady, Sorr ? '

' Yes,' said I. 'She is a very estimable old queen of the Central Indian States, and they say she is fat. How on earth could she go to Benares without all the city knowing her palanquin ? '

' 'Twas the eternal foolishness av the naygur-man. They saw the palanquin lying loneful an' forlornsome, an' the beauty av ut, after Dearsley's men had dhropped ut and gone away, an' they gave ut the best name that occurred to thim. Quite right too. For aught we know the ould lady was thravellin'

incog—like me.   I'm glad to hear she's fat.   I was
no light weight mysilf, an' my men were mortial
anxious to dhrop me under a great big archway
promiscuously ornamented wid the most improper
carvin's an' cuttin's I iver saw.   Begad! they made
me blush—like a—like a Maharanee.'

'The temple of Prithi-Devi,' I murmured, remembering the monstrous horrors of that sculptured
archway at Benares.

'.Pretty Devilskins, savin' your presence, Sorr!
There was nothin' pretty about ut, except me.
'Twas all half dhark, an' whin the coolies left they
shut a big black gate behind av us, an' half a company av fat yellow priests began pully-haulin' the
palanquins into a dharker place yet—a big stone
hall full av pillars, an' gods, an' incense, an' all
manner av similar thruck.   The gate disconcerted
me, for I perceived I wud have to go forward to get
out, my retreat bein' cut off.   By the same token
a good priest makes a bad palanquin-coolie.   Begad!
they nearly turned me inside out draggin' the
palanquin to the temple.   Now the disposishin av
the forces inside was this way.   The Maharance av
Gokral-Seetarun—that was me—lay by the favour
av Providence on the far left flank behind the dhark
av a pillar carved with elephints' heads.   The
remainder av the palanquins was in a big half circle
facing in to the biggest, fattest, an' most amazin'
she-god that iver I dreamed av.   Her head ran up
into the black above us, an' her feet stuck out in the
light av a little fire av melted butter that a priest
was feedin' out av a butter-dish.   Thin a man began
to sing an' play on somethin' back in the dhark, an'

'twas a queer song. Ut made my hair lift on the
back av my neck. Thin the doors av all the palanquins slid back, an' the women bundled out. I saw
what I'll niver see again. 'Twas more glorious than
thransformations at a pantomime, for they was in
pink an' blue an' silver an' red an' grass green, wid
dimonds an' imralds an' great red rubies all over
thim. But that was the least part av the glory. O
bhoys, they were more lovely than the like av any
loveliness in hiven ; ay, their little bare feet were
better than the white hands av a lord's lady, an'
their mouths were like puckered roses, an' their eyes
were bigger an' dharker than the eyes av any
livin' women I've seen. Ye may laugh, but I'm
speakin' truth. I niver saw the like, an' niver I will
again.'

'Seeing that in all probability you were watching
the wives and daughters of most of the kings of
India, the chances are that you won't,' I said, for
it was dawning on me that Mulvaney had stumbled
upon a big Queens' Praying at Benares.

'I niver will,' he said mournfully. 'That sight
doesn't come twist to any man. It made me
ashamed to watch. A fat priest knocked at my
door. I didn't think he'd have the insolince to
disturb the Maharance av Gokral-Seetarun, so I
lay still. "The old cow's asleep," sez he to another.
"Let her be," sez that. "'Twill be long before she
has a calf!" I might ha' known before he spoke
that all a woman prays for in Injia—an' for matter
o' that in England too—is childher. That made
me more sorry I'd come, me bein' as you well know,
a childless man.'

He was silent for a moment, thinking of his little son, dead many years ago.

'They prayed, an' the butter-fires blazed up an' the incense turned everything blue, an' between that an' the fires the women looked as tho' they were all ablaze an' twinklin'. They took hold av the she-god's knees, they cried out an' they threw themselves about, an' that world-without-end-amen music was dhrivin' thim mad. Mother av Hiven! how they cried, an' the ould she-god grinnin' above thim all so scornful! The dhrink was dyin' out in me fast, an' I was thinkin' harder than the thoughts wud go through my head—thinkin' how to get out, an' all manner of nonsense as well. The women were rockin' in rows, their di'mond belts clickin', an' the tears runnin' out betune their hands, an' the lights were goin' lower an' dharker. Thin there was a blaze like lightnin' from the roof, an' that showed me the inside av the palanquin, an' at the end where my foot was, stood the livin' spit an' image o' mysilf worked on the linin'. This man here, ut was.'

He hunted in the folds of his pink cloak, ran a hand under one, and thrust into the firelight a foot-long embroidered presentment of the great god Krishna, playing on a flute. The heavy jowl, the staring eye, and the blue-black moustache of the god made up a far-off resemblance to Mulvaney.

'The blaze was gone in a wink, but the whole schame came to me thin. I believe I was mad too. I slid the off-shutter open an' rowled out into the dhark behind the elephint-head pillar, tucked up my trousies to my knees, slipped off my boots an' tuk

'I was Krishna tootlin' on the flute.'—p.

a general hould av all the pink linin' av the palanquin.   Glory be, ut ripped out like a woman's dhriss
when you tread on ut at a sergeants' ball, an' a
bottle came with ut.   I tuk the bottle an' the next
minut I was out av the dhark av the pillar, the pink
linin' wrapped round me most graceful, the music
thunderin' like kettledrums, an' a could draught blowin'
round my bare legs.   By this hand that did ut, I
was Krishna tootlin' on the flute—the god that the
rig'mental chaplain talks about.   A sweet sight I
must ha' looked.   I knew my eyes were big, and
my face was wax-white, an' at the worst I must ha'
looked like a ghost.   But they took me for the livin'
god.   The music stopped, and the women were
dead dumb, an' I crooked my legs like a shepherd
on a china basin, an' I did the ghost-waggle with
my feet as I had done ut at the rig'mental theatre
many times, an' I slid acrost the width av that
temple in front av the she-god tootlin' on the beer
bottle.'

'Wot did you toot?' demanded Ortheris the
practical.

'Me?   Oh!'   Mulvaney sprang up, suiting the
action to the word, and sliding gravely in front of
us, a dilapidated but imposing deity in the half
light.   'I sang—

'Only say
You'll be Mrs. Brallaghan.
Don't say nay,
Charmin' Judy Callaghan.

I didn't know me own voice when I sang.   An' oh!
'twas pitiful to see the women.   The darlin's were
down on their faces.   Whin I passed the last wan

I cud see her poor little fingers workin' one in another as if she wanted to touch my feet. So I dhrew the tail av this pink overcoat over her head for the greater honour, an' I slid into the dhark on the other side av the temple, and fetched up in the arms av a big fat priest. All I wanted was to get away clear. So I tuk him by his greasy throat an' shut the speech out av him. "Out!" sez I. "Which way, ye fat heathen?"—"Oh!" sez he. "Man," sez I. "White man, soldier man, common soldier man. Where in the name av confusion is the back door?" The women in the temple were still on their faces, an' a young priest was holdin' out his arms above their heads.

'"This way," sez my fat friend, duckin' behind a big bull-god an' divin' into a passage. Thin I remimbered that I must ha' made the miraculous reputation av that temple for the next fifty years. "Not so fast," I sez, an' I held out both my hands wid a wink. That ould thief smiled like a father. I tuk him by the back av the neck in case he should be wishful to put a knife into me un-beknowst, an' I ran him up an' down the passage twice to collect his sensibilities! "Be quiet," sez he, in English. "Now you talk sense," I sez. "Fwhat'll you give me for the use av that most iligant palanquin I have no time to take away?"— "Don't tell," sez he. "Is ut like?" sez I. "But ye might give me my railway fare. I'm far from my home an' I've done you a service." Bhoys, 'tis a good thing to be a priest. The ould man niver throubled himself to dhraw from a bank. As I will prove to you subsequint, he philandered all

round the slack av his clothes an' began dribblin'
ten-rupee notes, old gold mohurs, and rupees into
my hand till I could hould no more.'

'You lie!' said Ortheris. 'You're mad or sunstrook. A native don't give coin unless you cut it
out o' 'im. 'Tain't nature.'

'Then my lie an' my sunstroke is concealed under
that lump av sod yonder,' retorted Mulvaney unruffled,
nodding across the scrub. 'An' there's a dale more
in nature than your squidgy little legs have iver
taken you to, Orth'ris, me son. Four hundred an'
thirty-four rupees by my reckonin', *an'* a big fat
gold necklace that I took from him as a remim-
brancer, was our share in that business.'

'An' 'e give it you for love?' said Ortheris.

'We were alone in that passage. Maybe I was
a trifle too pressin', but considher fwhat I had done
for the good av the temple and the iverlastin' joy
av those women. 'Twas cheap at the price. I wud
ha' taken more if I cud ha' found ut. I turned the
ould man upside down at the last, but he was milked
dhry. Thin he opened a door in another passage
an' I found mysilf up to my knees in Benares river-
water, an' bad smellin' ut is. More by token I had
come out on the river-line close to the burnin' ghat
and contagious to a cracklin' corpse. This was in
the heart av the night, for I had been four hours in
the temple. There was a crowd av boats tied up,
so I tuk wan an' wint across the river. Thin I
came home acrost country, lyin' up by day.'

'How on earth did you manage?' I said.

'How did Sir Frederick Roberts get from Cabul
to Candahar? He marched an' he niver tould how

near he was to breakin' down. That's why he is
fwhat he is. An' now—' Mulvaney yawned por-
tentously. 'Now I will go an' give myself up for
absince widout leave. It's eight-an'-twenty days an'
the rough end of the Colonel's tongue in orderly
room, any way you look at ut. But 'tis cheap at
the price.'

'Mulvaney,' said I softly. 'If there happens to
be any sort of excuse that the Colonel can in any
way accept, I have a notion that you'll get nothing
more than the dressing-down. The new recruits are
in, and——'

'Not a word more, Sorr. Is ut excuses the old
man wants? 'Tis not my way, but he shall have
thim. I'll tell him I was engaged in financial operations connected wid a church,' and he flapped his
way to cantonments and the cells, singing lustily—

> ' So they sent a corp'ril's file,
> And they put me in the gyard-room
> For conduck unbecomin' of a soldier.'

And when he was lost in the mist of the moonlight we could hear the refrain—

> ' Bang upon the big drum, bash upon the cymbals,
> As we go marchin' along, boys, oh !
> For although in this campaign
> There's no whisky nor champagne,
> We'll keep our spirits goin' with a song, boys !'

Therewith he surrendered himself to the joyful
and almost weeping guard, and was made much of
by his fellows. But to the Colonel he said that he
had been smitten with sunstroke and had lain in-

sensible on a villager's cot for untold hours ; and between laughter and goodwill the affair was smoothed over, so that he could, next day, teach the new recruits how to ' Fear God, Honour the Queen, Shoot Straight, and Keep Clean.'

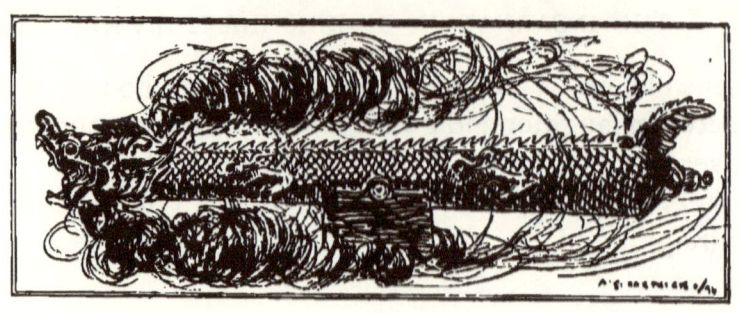

THE TAKING OF LUNGTUNGPEN

So we loosed a bloomin' volley,
  An' we made the beggars cut,
An' when our pouch was emptied out,
  We used the bloomin' butt,
      Ho! My!
      Don't yer come anigh,
When Tommy is a playin' with the baynit an' the butt.
          Barrack Room Ballad.

My friend Private Mulvaney told me this, sitting on the parapet of the road to Dagshai, when we were hunting butterflies together. He had theories about the Army, and coloured clay pipes perfectly. He said that the young soldier is the best to work with, 'on account av the surpassing innocinse av the child.'

'Now, listen!' said Mulvaney, throwing himself full length on the wall in the sun. 'I'm a born scutt av the barrick-room! The Army's mate an' dhrink to me, bekaze I'm wan av the few than can't quit ut. I've put in sivinteen ycars, an' the pipe-clay's in the marrow av me. Av I cud have kept out av wan big dhrink a month, I wud have been a Hon'ry Lift'nint by this time—a nuisince to my betthers, a laughin'-shtock to my equils, an' a curse to meself. Bein' fwhat I am, I'm Privit Mulvaney, wid no good-conduc' pay an' a devourin' thirst. Always barrin' me little frind Bobs Bahadur, I know as much about the Army as most men.'

I said something here.

'Wolseley be shot! Betune you an' me an' that butterfly net, he's a ramblin', incoherint sort av a divil, wid wan oi on the Quane an' the Coort, an' the other on his blessed silf—everlastin'ly playing Saysar an' Alexandrier rowled into a lump. Now Bobs is a sensible little man. Wid Bobs an' a few three-year-olds, I'd swape any army av the earth into a towel, an' throw it away afterwards. Faith, I'm not jokin'! 'Tis the bhoys—the raw bhoys—that don't know fwhat a bullut manes, an' wudn't care av they did—that dhu the work. They're crammed wid bull-mate till they fairly *ramps* wid good livin'; and thin, av they don't fight, they blow each other's hids off. 'Tis the trut' I'm tellin' you. They shud be kept on water an' rice in the hot weather; but there'd be a mut'ny av 'twas done.

'Did ye iver hear how Privit Mulvaney tuk the town av Lungtungpen? I thought not! 'Twas the Lift'nint got the credit; but 'twas me planned the schame. A little before I was inviladed from Burma, me an' four-an'-twenty young wans undher a Lift'nint Brazenose was ruinin' our dijeshins thryin' to catch dacoits. An' such double-ended divils I niver knew! 'Tis only a *dah* an' a Snider that makes a dacoit. Widout thim, he's a paceful culti-vator, an' felony for to shoot. We hunted, an' we hunted, an' tuk fever an' elephints now an' again; but no dacoits. Evenshually, we *puckarowed* wan man. "Trate him tinderly," sez the Lift'nint. So I tuk him away into the jungle, wid the Burmese Interprut'r an' my clanln'-rod. Sez I to the man, "My paceful squireen," sez I, "you shquot on your hunkers an' dimonstrate to *my* frind here, whcre *your* frinds are whin they're at home?" Wid that I intro-juced him to the clanin'-rod, an' he comminst to jabber; the Interprut'r interprutin' in betweens, an' me helpin' the Intilligince Departmint wid my clanin'-rod whin the man misremimbered.

'Prisintly, I learn that, acrost the river, about nine miles away, was a town just dhrippin' wid dahs, an' bohs an' arrows, an' dacoits, an' elephints, an' *jingles.* "Good!" sez I; "this office will now close!"

'That night, I went to the Lift'nint an' communi-cates my information. I never thought much of Lift'nint Brazenose till that night. He was shtiff wid books an' the-ouries, an' all manner av thrim-min's no manner av use. "Town did ye say?" sez he. "Accordin' to the the-ouries av War, we shud wait for reinforcemints."—"Faith!" thinks I, "we'd betther dig our graves thin;" for the nearest throops was up to their shtocks in the marshes out Mimbu way. "But," says the Lift'nint, "since 'tis a speshil case, I'll make an excepshin. We'll visit this Lung-tungpen to-night."

'The bhoys was fairly woild wid deloight whin I tould 'em; an', by this an' that, they wint through the jungle like buck-rabbits. About midnight we come to the shtrame which I had clane forgot to minshin to my orficer. I was on, ahead, wid four bhoys, an' I thought that the Lift'nint might want

' "Shtrip, bhoys," sez I.   "Shtrip to the buff, an' shwim in where glory
waits!" '—P. 157.

to the-ourise. " Shtrip, bhoys," sez I. " Shtrip to
the buff, an' shwim in where glory waits ! "—" But I
can't shwim ! " sez two av thim. " To think I should
live to hear that from a bhoy wid a board-school
edukashin ! " sez I. " Take a lump av thimber, an'
me an' Conolly here will ferry ye over, ye young
ladies ! "

' We got an ould tree-trunk, an' pushed off wid
the kits an' the rifles on it. The night was chokin'
dhark, an' just as we was fairly embarked, I heard
the Lift'nint behind av me callin' out. " There's a
bit av a *nullah* here, Sorr," sez I, " but I can feel the
bottom already." So I cud, for I was not a yard
from the bank.

' " Bit av a *nullah* ! Bit av an eshtuary ! " sez the
Lift'nint. " Go on, ye mad Irishman ! Shtrip,
bhoys ! " I heard him laugh ; an' the bhoys began
shtrippin' an' rollin' a log into the wather to put
their kits on. So me an' Conolly shtruck out through
the warm wather wid our log, an' the rest come on
behind.

' That shtrame was miles woide ! Orth'ris, on
the rear-rank , log, whispers we had got into the
Thames below Sheerness by mistake. " Kape , on
shwimmin', ye little blayguard," sez I, " an' don't go
pokin' your dirty jokes at the Irriwaddy."—" Silince,
men ! " sings out the Lift'nint. So we shwum on
into the black dhark, wid our chests on the logs,
trustin' in the Saints an' the luck av the British
Army.

' Evenshually, we hit ground—a bit av sand—an'
a man. I put my heel on the back av him. He
skreeched an' ran.

'"*Now* we've done it!" sez Lift'nint Brazenose. "Where the Divil *is* Lungtungpen?" There was about a minute and a half to wait. The bhoys laid a hould av their rifles an' some thried to put their belts on; we was marchin' wid fixed baynits av coorse. Thin we knew where Lungtungpen was; for we had hit the river-wall av it in the dhark, an' the whole town blazed wid thim messin' *jingles* an' Sniders like a cat's back on a frosty night. They was firin' all ways at wanst; but over our hids into the shtrame.

'"Have you got your rifles?" says Brazenose. "Got 'em!" sez Orth'ris. "I've got that thief Mulvaney's for all my back-pay, an' she'll kick my heart sick wid that blunderin' long shtock av hers."—"Go on!" yells Brazenose, whippin' his sword out. "Go on an' take the town! An' the Lord have mercy on our sowls!"

'Thin the bhoys gave wan divastatin' howl, an' pranced into the dhark, feelin' for the town, an' blindin' an' stiffin' like Cavalry Ridin' Masters whin the grass pricked their bare legs. I hammered wid the butt at some bamboo-thing that felt wake, an' the rest come an' hammered contagious, while the *jingles* was jingling, an' feroshus yells from inside was shplittin' our ears. We was too close under the wall for thim to hurt us.

'Evenshually, the thing, whatever ut was, bruk; an' the six-and-twinty av us tumbled, wan after the other, naked as we was borrun, into the town of Lungtungpen. There was a *melly* av a sumpshus kind for a whoile; but whether they tuk us, all white an' wet, for a new breed av divil, or a new kind av

'There was a *melly* av a sumpshus kind for a whoile.'—P. 158.

dacoit, I don't know. They ran as though we was both, an' we wint into thim, baynit an' butt, shrickin' wid laughin'. There was torches in the shtreets, an' I saw little Orth'ris rubbin' his showlther iv ry time he loosed my long-shtock Martini ; an' Brazenose walkin' into the gang wid his sword, like Diarmid av the Gowlden Collar—barring he hadn't a stitch av clothin' on him. We diskivered elephints wid dacoits under their bellies, an', what wid wan thing an' another, we was busy till mornin' takin' possession av the town of Lungtungpen.

'Thin we halted an' formed up, the wimmen howlin' in the houses an' Lift'nint Brazenose blushin' pink in the light av the mornin' sun. 'Twas the most ondasint p'rade I iver tuk a hand in. Foive-and-twenty privits an' an orficer av the Line in review ordher, an' not as much as wud dust a fife betune 'em all in the way of clothin'! Eight av us had their belts an' pouches on ; but the rest had gone in wid a handful av cartridges an' the skin God gave thim. *They* was as nakid as Vanus.

'"Number off from the right!" sez the Lift'nint. "Odd numbers fall out to dress; even numbers pathrol the town till relieved by the dressing party." Let me tell you, pathrollin' a town wid nothing on is an ex*pay*rience. I pathrolled for tin minutes, an' begad, before 'twas over, I blushed. The women laughed so. I niver blushed before or since ; but I blushed all over my carkiss thin. Orth'ris didn't pathrol. He sez only, "Portsmith Barricks an' the 'Ard av a Sunday!" Thin he lay down an' rowled any ways wid laughin'.

'Whin we was all dhressed, we counted the dead

—sivinty-foive dacoits besides wounded. We tuk five elephints, a hunder' an' sivinty Sniders, two hunder' dahs, and a lot av other burglarious thruck. Not a man av us was hurt—excep' maybe the Lift'nint, an' he from the shock to his dasincy.

'The Headman av Lungtungpen, who surrinder'd himself, asked the Interprut'r—"Av the English fight like that wid their clo'es off, what in the wurruld do they do wid their clo'es on?" Orth'ris began rowlin' his eyes an' crackin' his fingers an' dancin' a step-dance for to impress the Headman. He ran to his house; an' we spint the rest av the day carryin' the Lift'nint on our showlthers round the town, an' playin' wid the Burmese babies—fat, little, brown little divils, as pretty as picturs.

'Whin I was inviladed for the dysent'ry to India, I sez to the Lift'nint, "Sorr," sez I, "you've the makin's in you av a great man; but, av you'll let an ould sodger spake, you're too fond of the-ourisin'." He shuk hands wid me and sez, "Hit high, hit low, there's no plasin' you, Mulvaney. You've seen me waltzin' through Lungtungpen like a Red Injin widout the war-paint, an' you say I'm too fond av the-ourisin'?"—"Sorr," sez I, for I loved the bhoy; "I wud waltz wid you in that condishin through *Hell*, an' so wud the rest av the men!" Thin I wint downshtrame in the flat an' left him my blessin'. May the Saints carry ut where ut should go, for he was a fine upstandin' young orficer.

'To reshume. Fwhat I've said jist shows the use av three-year-olds. Wud fifty seasoned sodgers have taken Lungtungpen in the dhark that way? No! They'd know the risk av fever and chill. Let alone the shootin'. Two hunder' might have done ut. But the three-year-olds know little an' care less ; an' where there's no fear, there's no danger. Catch thim young, feed thim high, an' by the honour av that great little man Bobs, behind a good orficer 'tisn't only dacoits they'd smash wid their clo'es off——'tis Con-ti-nental Ar-r-r-mies! They tuk Lungtungpen nakid ; an' they'd take St. Pethersburg in their dhrawers! Begad, they would that!

' Here's your pipe, Sorr. Shmoke her tinderly wid honey-dew, afther letting the reek av the Canteen plug die away. But 'tis no good, thanks to you all the same, fillin' my pouch wid your chopped hay. Canteen baccy's like the Army. It shpoils a man's taste for moilder things.'

So saying, Mulvaney took up his butterfly-net, and returned to barracks.

THE MADNESS OF PRIVATE ORTHERIS

Oh ! Where would I be when my froat was dry?
Oh ! Where would I be when the bullets fly?
Oh ! Where would I be when I come to die?
　　Why,
Somewheres anigh my chum.
　If 'e's liquor 'e'll give me some,
　If I'm dyin' 'e'll 'old my 'ead,
　An' 'e'll write 'em 'Ome when I'm dead.—
　Gawd send us a trusty chum !

Barrack Room Ballad.

MY friends Mulvaney and Ortheris had gone on a shooting expedition for one day. Learoyd was still in hospital, recovering from fever picked up in Burma. They sent me an invitation to join them, and were genuinely pained when I brought beer—almost enough beer to satisfy two Privates of the Line—and Me.

' 'Twasn't for that we bid you welkim, Sorr,' said Mulvaney sulkily. ' 'Twas for the pleasure av your comp'ny.'

Ortheris came to the rescue with—' Well, 'e won't be none the worse for bringin' liquor with 'im. We ain't a file o' Dooks. We're bloomin' Tommies, ye

Ortheris heaved a big sigh. —P. 163.

cantankris Hirishman ; an'· 'cre's your very good 'ealth ! '

We shot all the forenoon, and killed two pariah-dogs, four green parrots, sitting, one kite by the burning-ghaut, one snake flying, one mud-turtle, and eight crows. Game was plentiful. Then we sat down to tiffin—'bull-mate an' bran bread,' Mulvaney called it—by the side of the river, and took pot shots at the crocodiles in the intervals of cutting up the food with our only pocket-knife. Then we drank up all the beer, and threw the bottles into the water and fired at them. After that, we eased belts and stretched ourselves on the warm sand and smoked. We were too lazy to continue shooting.

Ortheris heaved a big sigh, as he lay on his stomach with his head between his fists. Then he swore quietly into the blue sky.

'Fwhat's that for?' said Mulvaney. 'Have ye, not drunk enough?'

'Tott'nim Court Road, an' a gal I·fancied there. Wot's the good of sodgerin'?'

'Orth'ris, me son,' said Mulvaney hastily, ''tis more than likely you've got throuble in your inside wid the beer. I feel that way mesilf whin my liver gets rusty.'

Ortheris went on slowly, not heeding the interruption—

'I'm a Tommy—a bloomin', eight-anna, dog-stealin' Tommy, with a number instead of a, decent name. Wot's the good o' me? If I 'ad a stayed at 'Ome, I might a married that gal and a kep' a little shorp in the 'Ammersmith 'Igh.—"S. Orth'ris, Prac-ti-cal Taxi-der-mist." With a stuff' fox, like they 'as in the Haylesbury Dairies, in the winder, an' a little case of blue and yaller glass-heyes, an' a little wife to call " shorp ! " " shorp ! " when the door-bell rung. As it *his*, I'm on'y a Tommy—a Bloomin', Gawd - forsaken, Beer - swillin' Tommy. " Rest on your harms—'*versed*. Stan' at—*hease ;* '*Shun*. 'Verse — *harms*. Right an' lef' — *tarrn*. Slow—*march*. 'Alt—*front*. Rest on your harms —'*versed*. With blank-cartridge—*load*." An' that's the end o' me.' He was quoting fragments from Funeral Parties' Orders.

' Stop ut ! ' shouted Mulvaney. ' Whin you've fired into nothin' as often as me, over a better man than yoursilf, you will not make a mock av thim orders. 'Tis worse than whistlin' the *Dead March* in barricks. An' you full as a tick, an' the sun cool, an' all an' all ! I take shame for you. You're no better than a Pagin—you an' your firin'-parties an' your glass-eyes. Won't *you* stop ut, Sorr ? '

What could I do ? Could I tell Ortheris any-thing that he did not know of the pleasures of his life ? I was not a Chaplain nor a Subaltern, and Ortheris had a right to speak as he thought fit.

' Let him run, Mulvaney,' I said. ' It's the beer.'

' No ! ' ' 'Tisn't the beer,' said Mulvaney. ' I know fwhat's comin'. He's tuk this way now an' agin, an' it's bad—it's bad—for I'm fond av the bhoy.'

Indeed, Mulvaney seemed needlessly anxious ; but I knew that he looked after Ortheris in a fatherly way.

' Let me talk, let me talk,' said Ortheris dreamily. ' D'you stop your parrit screamin' of a 'ot day, when

the cage is a-cookin' 'is pore little pink toes orf,
Mulvaney?'

'Pink toes!   D'ye mane to say you've pink toes
undher your bullswools, ye blandanderin','—Mulvaney
gathered himself together for a terrific denunciation
—'school-misthress!   Pink toes!   How much Bass
wid the label did that ravin' child dhrink?'

''Tain't Bass,' said Ortheris.   'It's a bitterer beer
nor that.   It's 'ome-sickness!'

'Hark to him!   An' he goin' Home in the
Sherapis in the inside av four months!'

'I don't care.   It's all one to me.   'Ow d'you
know I ain't 'fraid o' dyin' 'fore I gets my discharge
paipers?'   He recommenced, in a sing-song voice,
the Orders.

I had never seen this side of Ortheris's character
before, but evidently Mulvaney had, and attached
serious importance to it.   While Ortheris babbled,
with his head on his arms, Mulvaney whispered to
me—

'He's always tuk this way whin he's been checked
overmuch by the childher they make Sargints nowa-
days.   That an' havin' nothin' to do.   I can't make
ut out anyways.'

'Well, what does it matter?   Let him talk himself through.'

Ortheris began singing a parody of 'The Ramrod
Corps,' full of cheerful allusions to battle, murder,
and sudden death.   He looked out across the river
as he sang; and his face was quite strange to me.
Mulvaney caught me by the elbow to ensure attention.

'Matther?   It matthers everything!   'Tis some

sort av fit that's on him. I've seen ut. 'Twill hould him all this night, an' in the middle av it he'll get out av his cot an' go rakin' in the rack for his 'courtremints. Thin he'll come over to me an' say, "I'm goin' to Bombay. Answer for me in the mornin'." Thin me an' him will fight as we've done before—him to go an' me to hould him—an' so we'll both come on the books for disturbin' in barricks. I've belted him, an' I've bruk his head, an' I've talked to him, but 'tis no manner av use whin the fit's on him. He's as good a bhoy as ever stepped whin his mind's clear. I know fwhat's comin', though, this night in barricks. Lord send he doesn't loose on me whin I rise to knock him down. 'Tis that that's in my mind day an' night.'

This put the case in a much less pleasant light, and fully accounted for Mulvaney's anxiety. He seemed to be trying to coax Ortheris out of the fit; for he shouted down the bank where the boy was lying—

'Listen now, you wid the "pore pink toes" an' the glass-eyes! Did you shwim the Irriwaddy at night, behin' me, as a bhoy shud; or were you hidin' under a bed, as you was at Ahmid Kheyl?'

This was at once a gross insult and a direct lie, and Mulvaney meant it to bring on a fight. But Ortheris seemed shut up in some sort of trance. He answered slowly, without a sign of irritation, in the same cadenced voice as he had used for his firing-party orders—

'*Hi* swum the Irriwaddy in the night, as you know, for to take the town of Lungtungpen, nakid an' without fear. *Hand* where I was at Ahmed

Kheyl you know, and four bloomin' Paythans know
too.   But that was summat to do, an' I didn't think
o' dyin'.   Now I'm sick to go 'Ome—go 'Ome—go
'Ome !   No, I ain't mammysick, because my uncle
brung me up, but I'm sick for London again ; sick
for the sounds of 'er, an' the sights of 'er, and the
stinks of 'er ;   orange-peel and hasphalte an' gas
comin' in over Vaux'all Bridge.   Sick for the rail
goin' down to Box 'Ill, with your gal on your knee
an' a new clay pipe in your face.   That, an' the
Stran' lights where you knows ev'ry one, an' the
Copper that takes you up is a old friend that tuk
you up before, when you was a little, smitchy boy
lying loose 'tween the Temple an' the Dark Harches.
No bloomin' guard-mountin', no bloomin' rotten-
stone, nor khaki, an' yourself your own master with
a gal to take an' see the Humaners practisin' a-
hookin' dead corpses out of the Serpentine o' Sun-
days.   An' I lef' all that for to serve the Widder
beyond the seas, where there ain't no women and
there ain't no liquor worth 'avin', and there ain't
nothin' to see, nor do, nor say, nor feel, nor think.
Lord love you, Stanley Orth'ris, but you're a bigger
bloomin' fool than the rest o' the reg'ment and
Mulvaney wired together !   There's the Widder
sittin' at 'Ome with a gold crownd on 'er 'ead ; and
'ere am Hi, Stanley Orth'ris, the Widder's property,
a rottin' FOOL !'

His voice rose at the end of the sentence, and he
wound up with a six-shot Anglo-Vernacular oath.
Mulvaney said nothing, but looked at me as if he
expected that I could bring peace to poor Ortheris's
troubled brain.

I remembered once at Rawal Pindi having seen a man, nearly mad with drink, sobered by being made a fool of. Some regiments may know what I mean. I hoped that we might slake off Ortheris in the same way, though he was perfectly sober. So I said—

'What's the use of grousing there, and speaking against The Widow?'

'I didn't!' said Ortheris. 'S'elp me, Gawd, I never said a word agin 'er, an' I wouldn't—not if I was to desert this minute!'

Here was my opening. 'Well, you meant to, anyhow. What's the use of cracking-on for nothing? Would you slip it now if you got the chance?'

'On'y try me!' said Ortheris, jumping to his feet as if he had been stung.

Mulvaney jumped too. 'Fwhat are you going to do?' said he.

. 'Help Ortheris down to Bombay or Karachi, whichever he likes. You can report that he separated from you before tiffin, and left his gun on the bank here!'

'I'm to report that—am I?' said Mulvaney slowly. 'Very well. If Orth'ris manes to desert now, and will desert now, an' you, Sorr, who have been a frind to me an' to him, will help him to ut, I, Terence Mulvaney, on my oath which I've never bruk yet, will report as you say. But——' here he stepped up to Ortheris, and shook the stock of the fowling-piece in his face — 'your fistes help you, Stanley Orth'ris, if ever I come across you agin!'

'I don't care!' said Ortheris. 'I'm sick o' this

dorg's life. Give me a chanst. Don't play with me.
Le' me go !'

'Strip,' said I, 'and change with me, and then I'll
tell you what to do.'

I hoped that the absurdity of this would check
Ortheris; but he had kicked off his ammunition-
boots and got rid of his tunic almost before I had
loosed my shirt-collar. Mulvaney gripped me by
the arm—

'The fit's on him : the fit's workin' on him still !
By my Honour and Sowl, we shall be accessiry to a
desartion yet. Only twenty-eight days, as you say,
Sorr, or fifty-six, but think o' the shame—the black
shame to him an' me !' I had never seen Mulvaney
so excited.

But Ortheris was quite calm, and, as soon as he
had exchanged clothes with me, and I stood up a
Private of the Line, he said shortly, 'Now! Come
on. What nex'? D'ye mean fair. What must I
do to get out o' this 'ere a-Hell?'

I told him that, if he would wait for two or three
hours near the river, I would ride into the Station
and come back with one hundred rupees. He would,
with that money in his pocket, walk to the nearest
side-station on the line, about five miles away, and
would there take a first-class ticket for Karachi.
Knowing that he had no money on him when he
went out shooting, his regiment would not immediately wire to the seaports, but would hunt for him
in the native villages near the river. Further, no
one would think of seeking a deserter in a first-class
carriage. At Karachi, he was to buy white clothes
and ship, if he could, on a cargo-steamer.

Here he broke in. If I helped him to Karachi, he would arrange all the rest. Then I ordered him to wait where he was until it was dark enough for me to ride into the station without my dress being noticed. Now God in His wisdom has made the heart of the British Soldier, who is very often an unlicked ruffian, as soft as the heart of a little child, in order that he may believe in and follow his officers into tight and nasty places. He does not so readily come to believe in a 'civilian,' but, when he does, he believes implicitly and like a dog. I had had the honour of the friendship of Private Ortheris, at intervals, for more than three years, and we had dealt with each other as man by man. Consequently, he considered that all my words were true, and not spoken lightly.

Mulvaney and I left him in the high grass near the river-bank, and went away, still keeping to the high grass, towards my horse. The shirt scratched me horribly.

We waited nearly two hours for the dusk to fall and allow me to ride off. We spoke of Ortheris in whispers, and strained our ears to catch any sound from the spot where we had left him. But we heard nothing except the wind in the plume-grass.

'I've bruk his head,' said Mulvaney earnestly, 'time an' agin. I've nearly kilt him wid the belt, an' *yet* I can't knock thim fits out av his soft head. No! An' he's not soft, for he's reasonable an' likely by natur'. Fwhat is ut? Is ut his breedin' which is nothin', or his edukashin which he niver got? You that think ye know things, answer me that.'

But I found no answer. I was wondering how

We set off at the double and found him plunging about wildly through the grass.—P. 171.

long Ortheris, in the bank of the river, would hold out, and whether I should be forced to help him to desert, as I had given my word.

Just as the dusk shut down and, with a very heavy heart, I was beginning to saddle up my horse, we heard wild shouts from the river.

The devils had departed from Private Stanley Ortheris, No. 22639, B Company. The loneliness, the dusk, and the waiting had driven them out as I had hoped. We set off at the double and found him plunging about wildly through the grass, with his coat off—my coat off, I mean. He was calling for us like a madman.

When we reached him he was dripping with perspiration, and trembling like a startled horse. We had great difficulty in soothing him. He complained that he was in civilian kit, and wanted to tear my clothes off his body. I ordered him to strip, and we made a second exchange as quickly as possible.

The rasp of his own 'grayback' shirt and the squeak of his boots seemed to bring him to himself. He put his hands before his eyes and said—

'Wot was it? I ain't mad, I ain't sunstrook, an' I've bin an' gone an' said, an' bin an' gone an' done—— *Wot* 'ave I bin an' done!'

'Fwhat have you done?' said Mulvaney. 'You've dishgraced yourself—though that's no matter. You've dishgraced B Comp'ny, an' worst av all, you've dishgraced *Me!* Me that taught you how for to walk abroad like a man—whin you was a dhirty little, fish-backed little, whimperin' little recruity. As you are now, Stanley Orth'ris!'

Ortheris said nothing for a while. Then he un-
slung his belt, heavy with the badges of half a dozen
regiments that his own had lain with, and handed it
over to Mulvaney.

'I'm too little for to mill you, Mulvaney,' said he,
'an' you've strook me before ; but you can take an'
cut me in two with this 'ere if you like.'

Mulvaney turned to me.

'Lave me to talk to him, Sorr,' said Mulvaney.

I left, and on my way home thought a good deal
over Ortheris in particular, and my friend Private
Thomas Atkins whom I love, in general.

But I could not come to any conclusion of any
kind whatever.

Printed by R. & R. CLARK, LIMITED, *Edinburgh.*